BROTHERHOOD

OF

SECRETS

JC ROMALION (ROM)

PublishAmerica
Baltimore

First printing

This is a work of fiction. Names, characters, places, and incidents either are the product of the author's imagination or are used fictitiously. Any resemblance to actual persons, living or dead, events, or locales is entirely coincidental.

PublishAmerica has allowed this work to remain exactly as the author intended, verbatim, without editorial input.

ISBN: 1-60474-802-8
PUBLISHED BY PUBLISHAMERICA, LLLP
www.publishamerica.com
Baltimore

Printed in the United States of America

To
Laura
From
Jc Romalion

CHAPTER I

A day of new beginnings, resolutions and dreams are made and broken. New Years day, when most of us have promises of better things in the New Year, resolutions are made and then broken. Like a lot of other broken promises in life along the way. Most of us have those aspirations, but always seem to fall short.

Cal Rushton didn't have any of those illusions. For him it would be another year of setbacks, defeats and bitterness. It seemed like everything he attempted ended in failure, disappointment and pain. He decided a few

Month's prior to this fateful moment to give it all up. In other words this new day of the New Year he would take control.

Cal was angry at the world. He was angry at all the disappointments and failures in his life. He decided rather than fight to make it better, he would end the struggle. After all he had nothing to live for. He had a mundane job that was going nowhere. His high school friends had long ago moved on with their lives. Most of them were now married with children and were successful to some degree. Every relationship Cal had been in ended in bitterness, deception and lies. He felt his life meant nothing to him anymore. He could think of no reason, one person that would miss him. The timing seemed right to him, that he should choose this day to end it all.

Others wouldn't understand why he would want to do such a thing, life is so precious and short, make every moment count. He had heard that before, most of those people he figured just had their heads buried in the sand. He had mentioned to his doctor, and the doctor suggested psychiatric evaluation. Cal went to the shrink, thinking that it wouldn't matter anyway, but he would humor him and try to please the man. That was almost four years ago. Although, it seemed to help him at the time, a couple months past and he had the same suicidal thoughts emerging again.

Others looked at Cal as a roughneck with emotional problems. Even his current girlfriend Eva had found him abrasive and rough.

No one could understand him and his beliefs and disbelieves, if he truly had any at all. Eva had threatened to break off their 6-month relationship on numerous occasions. Cal lived life on the edge with drug addiction, alcohol abuse and womanizing. His old friends often dodged him not wanting much to do with him. More people rejected him, including his own family.

There was on exception however, his brother Bobby. He picked up the old chrome chair in the cluttered kitchen. The dishes were piled up on the counter, food left out to rot, garbage cans overflowed onto the floor. Fruit flies buzzed in delight over the treats left by him.

He moved the chair into the shabbily decorated living room. His apartment looked like someone else's garbage. His lifestyle had only reinforced that he had serious problems. Even his attire reflected a man that didn't care anymore. The torn, shaggy, unwashed clothes only coincided with the unkempt beard. His living room was also his bedroom, ashtrays overflowed; instead of emptying them he butted them out on the floor.

He was a man without power, without self-esteem and dignity. He lacked any redeeming qualities; he was a social outcast from society. Even his job was suffering with his tardiness and obscene behavior. Cal had been given several warnings and finally on New Years Eve he ended that part of his life too. He beat his boss up, giving him two black eyes and a broken nose. He got fired, but that was his plan anyway.

He placed the chair in the center of the room below a huge beam that went across the room. He walked over to the closet of his shabby apartment, pulling out a rope. The rope made it clear that he planned this day. He tied the loose end of the rope securely to the post in the kitchen. He then flung the rope over the beam above the chair. He tugged on the rope making sure it was tight. He nodded his own approval; satisfied that he could at least do this right.

So this is what had become of his life. He was sure that this was the answer to all his problems. He stepped onto the seat of the wobbly chair, slipping the noose around his neck. His face was exempt from expression, cinching the noose tighter. He wondered how his life might have turned out differently, if he would have changed some things in his life. He stepped onto the back of the chair; it began teetering under his weight. He glanced out the front window of his apartment at the cruel world he lived in.

Why was his world so different and unforgiving than others? He had made a lot of mistakes he would be the first one to admit to that, but was it worth killing himself over. The sky was a crimson red, the sun now breaking through the clouds for this new day. Suddenly, he had a strange thought enter his mind. It was something her remembered from his childhood.

"Red sky in the morning, sailors take warning". The voice seemed vague in his mind.

Maybe, it was his father's voice; he couldn't remember much about his father. His father had died when he was a young boy. His eyes watered now at the thought of his father. Maybe, if his father had lived longer things might have been different. He looked out the window watching a young boy scampering down the road.

He thought about what people would say about him. They wouldn't even remember him a year down the road. His own brother, Bobby, would more than likely call him a coward and a loser. What about those that did care, he could count them on his one hand. He had alienated himself from the rest of the world shutting down from the rest of the population.

"Oh my God" Cal said to himself as he thought of those things now. The chair swayed under his feet slipping out from under him.

What if I can change things and start trying harder, I won't have anyone here that will care other than my brother and his wife. What if I stop taking drugs, drinking and go to an addiction clinic.

"I want to live and live right" he thought to himself "maybe, I can make a difference in someone's life. He grasped at the tight rope trying to loosen the noose. It was too late the noose had already begun to dig into to his neck. He pried with his fingers on the rope so hard he broke a fingernail off. He gripped at the rope realizing he was dangling in mid air. His eyes bulged in his head blood vessels popping in his eyes. He gulped for air, but there was none. He squirmed gasping for air.

Cal's last thoughts were "Oh my God please let me live".

It was to late his body went limp, as his struggle became fruitless. His hands fell to his sides, his life flashing before his eyes. His face turned purple, his eyes fogged over, the room grew dim.

"I told you, you were a loser" voices echoed in his head.

One last desperate gasp, the remaining impulses to grab the rope, his eyes were wide open a look of terror in them. He realized he didn't want to die anymore. Suddenly, he was floating above his lifeless body. Looking down at his body, confusion. "That's me": he tried to scream but no one heard him. He felt his body slowly turning in mid air, before suddenly plunging face forward towards the floor. His hands went out in reaction to protect him from the impact, but there was no impact. His eyes closed as he sensed the impact. No sudden jolt, no impact. He opened his eyes to total blackness, but he was still falling. He screamed the scream only in his mind.

He was alone now, as he had wanted. He was scared and wanted nothing more than to change his mind on dying. But, it was too late he was leaving his body and going to someplace cluttered with darkness.

"Is this what it's like to die?" he questioned himself.

He was still falling in the pitch black, echoes of his screams bounced back at him. A stench, an incredible, awful smell, lofted up to his nostrils. Was it sulfur, death, it burned his throat choking him. His eyes watered, his throat burned and still he screamed.

"I'm going to hell," he told himself.

Suddenly, without warning he stopped falling. It was still pitch black. Something sticky and damp was here; he could sense its presence. He felt wetness of the wall on his back. He reached forward trying to feel if there was something there. He took a step forward and again he was falling, screaming from his lungs, something grazed his shoulder. He shuttered at the though of something with him in the darkness. Where was he going, what kind of thing had he done to himself? He had a million questions and no one there to answer them. All the planning he had done, and at the last minute to change his mind. The feelings of wanting to live, wanting to change and wanting to start over didn't matter anymore he told himself.

Bobby Rushton was worried about his brother, and hadn't heard from him since Christmas Eve. He didn't hear anything on Christmas day and figured that Cal was so out of it he even forgot it was Christmas day. He left his house and headed over to Cal's apartment to see what was going on and to give him a piece of his mind.

Cal needed help, help that Bobby couldn't give him. He parked the car in the parking lot and looked up at the bare windows of Cal's apartment. He muttered that he was going to straighten him out on live and get the help for him he desperately needed.

Bobby saved Cal Rushton's life by going over there that day. Inside he found Cal's lifeless body swinging from a rope. Cal was still gasping for air, coughing and choking. Bobby ran to the kitchen grabbing a butcher knife to cut the rope. He sliced the rope several times before it finally broke free. Bobby who laid him on the floor caught Cal's limp body. Bobby was kneeling beside him in the middle of the room.

"What the fuck are you trying to do?" he shouted irately at Cal. "You want to die that bad?" he finished.

Bobby was vicious that Cal had tried to kill himself. Cal gasped trying to talk, his windpipe crushed by the rope. His eyes bulging and bloodshot, he was trying to tell Bobby that he really didn't want to die and he had changed his mind.

"Just shut to fuck up" Bobby spewed "there's an ambulance on the way"

"I don't want to die?" Cal squeaked finally getting the words out.

"You sure have a funny way of showing it" Bobby said rolling him onto his side.

The ambulance arrived working on Cal to get him to the hospital. He was near death when they arrived and they had to work on him quite awhile to get his vitals back to normal. He didn't remember much as he faded in and out of consciousness. He vaguely remembered the drive to the hospital. He remembered the men in the ambulance working on him to establish a clean airway. The next thing he knew it was morning. He awoke with restraints on his arms, to hold him down.

A nurse scurried about the room waking him. He didn't like the feeling of being restrained but it was for his own safety.

"Where am I?" he said barely a whisper coming out of him.

"Don't try to talk Mr. Rushton," the nurse warned, "your in the hospital."

"It's going to be awhile before you can talk again." She continued, "To much talking may damage your windpipe" she warned him again.

The nurse went about taking his pulse and blood pressure. He could feel the collar around his neck. A tube was inserted in his throat so he could breath. He was hooked up with tubes in his nose. He had done a lot of damage to himself.

He laid motionless thinking about what had happened. His near death experience had left him speechless and reassessing his life. He now knew that he had been given another opportunity to live again. Maybe, this time he could do it right. Maybe, now he could leave a mark on the world. He wanted something to be remembered by. Maybe, he could make amends with his family for doing such a terrible thing. The suicide attempt was only a blur on what had happened.

Cal wanted to move on in life, and to forget what had happened. But he also realized he would need help and support to get through what he had tried to do. He knew he needed help and needed to set goals for himself. He thought that part would be easy, but again, most do when the go through this type of ordeal. The nurse untied the restraints and gave him a notepad.

"Mr. Rushton would you like anything" she asked him handing him a pencil.

He handed her the note back. She read the note; she seemed amused at what was written.

He sounded like he wanted to start life over today that was brave but unadvisable until he was evaluated and reassessed.

"I'm sorry Mr. Rushton, you can't get out of bed until the doctor comes in to take the tubes out" she told him.

Again he scribbled something down, telling her he needed to get up and move around.

"Because Mr. Rushton you tried to kill yourself," the nurse said in a scolding manner.

She stood looking at him trying to decide whether to console him or scold him when the doctor walked in.

"Good morning" the doctor said addressing Cal.

"So Cal, you almost did it huh," the doctor said referring to his attempted suicide.

The overweight doctor asked the nurse how he was doing. She told him that he seemed to be doing fine, and that he had requested the intervenes tube be taken out. He looked Cal over as if he checking him out. The doctor was sweating and was a very heavy man. He huffed and puffed looking at Cal. The doctor moved to the other side of the bed looking down at Cal.

"Your not going to harm yourself again are you?" The doctor asked.

Doctor Moore was heavy he specialized in psychiatry. The doctor's heavy breathing was hard and deep. He acted and looked like he was going to take a heart attack at any moment. His face was red, his speckled beard and glasses suited his profession.

"I know you can't talk right now. So I'm going to talk for you," the doctor said staring down at him.

"You realize that you're considered a threat to yourself". "So I've recommended that you be moved to the fifth floor for evaluation," he told him waiting for a response.

"You will get the help you need there," the doctor commented.

Cal scribbled on the notepad handing it to the doctor. He knew what the fifth floor meant and he didn't want to go up there.

"I don't want to go up there, I've learned my lesson," the note said.

"Well, you really don't have a choice in the matter," the doctor scolded. "Your brother Bobby has signed the consent form authorizing us to do what is best," he said taking his clipboard and going out of the room.

Cal tried to sit up but felt Very light headed, slumping back down into the bed. Two big burly men appeared in his room. Before he knew what was going on, he was whisked away to the fifth floor. He drifted in and out of sleep. He was heavily medicated, but still he remembered having nightmares. These nightmares always had him falling into the darkness. He wondered if he had died and was making his way to somewhere beyond.

He had to make peace, escape his troubled past and live again. He knew he was a troubled soul, and up to now thought his life was meaningless. He knew he had to give up drugs, alcohol and fighting. He wondered about Eva his girlfriend. Would she dump him after this? Did she even know about his attempted suicide? He drifted back to sleep his dream this time started out nice.

He was in a field picking flowers for a beautiful woman. He didn't know who the woman was but she was there. They were holding hands, giggling, kissing and laughing. He felt a tremendous feeling of love. Without warning the dream turned violent. He was falling in that deep dark hole again. Falling, falling and falling, he could feel the pain, terror and agony, which tore at his soul. He awoke with the nurse shaking him. It was unexplainable the feeling he was having.

Cal was terrified of something but couldn't see in the darkness.

"Mr. Rushton, wake up," she said shaking him.

"Help," he muttered very low, still in his dream.

"You're having a nightmare Mr. Ruston" she tried to reassure him.

"It's okay Mr. Rushton, you're going to be fine," the nurse said calming him down.

Not long after that Cal was treated by the mental health specialist at the hospital and was transferred. He thought he would soon be able to go home and hopefully get on the right track with his life again. Cal was transferred to Cedar Hills Infirmary; doctors informed him that they thought he needed more psychiatric help with his mental stability. He didn't like the idea but was reassured that it would only be a week or two and then he would be released. He had enough of people trying to pick his brain apart to find out what he was thinking and going through. He had learned his lesson in his opinion and didn't need any more doctors prying in to his past and why he did what he did.

Bobby came to see him later that day at Cedar Hills. They talked briefly before Cal drifted off to sleep. He vaguely remembered Bobby's visit and was so out of it on pills he still couldn't think straight. He thought he was dreaming that Bobby was there and was unsure. He didn't remember being loaded into a wheelchair but when he awoke he was next to the window overlooking the grounds.

He sat looking out the window, he felt so strange sitting there. He watched the others milling around the lobby. They were doing different things and he felt like he was in the movie One Flew over the Cuckoo's Nest. One of the other patients came over towards him.

"Hi, my name is Beerrrnnniiee," the scrawny man stammered.

Cal didn't answer him; he didn't know how to react. He had always shied away from the mentally handicapped, they frightened him, and his fear was what if he was that way. He had a bad habit also of making fun of such individuals. He watched as the scrawny man hovered above him, the man's arms slightly deformed waving them around. He was looking at Cal very strange and watching him trying to get a reaction.

"You're new," he stammered staring at Cal.

He yammered on for several minutes about different patients and the menu items.

Finally, a nurse came over to inform Cal he had a visitor. When Cal finally saw his brother, tears welled up in his eyes. He hadn't been able to show his emotions in this way for a long time and it felt good. He felt trapped in here and felt that he didn't belong with the rest of the lunatics. He watched Bobby coming over and was happy to see him.

"Brother" Bobby said matter of fact pulling a chair next to the wheelchair.

"Thanks Bobby" Cal said referring to the fact he had saved his life.

The rope burn on his neck was very evident "For what?" Bobby asked him.

"For saving my life, and for always being here when I need you" Cal confessed.

"You stupid bastard" Bobby cursed, "Life is to short to end it that way," he said scolding his brother.

"I realize that now" Cal said a tone of regret in his voice.

Cal and Bobby talked awhile-exchanging stories about growing up together. They came from a family of 4 four. Cal was the eldest brother, Bobby the youngest. Most of the family had gone separate ways, only contacting each other once a year or so, mostly on holidays.

Their mother had remarried for the third time and moved to Florida. Cal didn't know his father very well; he died when Cal was eleven. They had two sisters Martha and Julia that they very rarely seen. Martha came to visit usually once a year.

Bobby had married Anne and they had two beautiful children together. After the conversation about the family and trivial things Bobby looked at the clock.

"Well got to get going Bro." Bobby said slapping his hand on Cal's leg.

"How long am I in here for?" Cal asked hoping the answer wouldn't be long.

"Probably only a couple days or so, until their sure your not going to try and kill yourself again" referring to the doctors orders.

Bobby got up from his chair heading for the door.

Cal sat watching him wanting to leave with him. He felt so alone in here and didn't want to stay any longer than he had to.

He hoped that his dreams would stop as well. Maybe, once he stopped taking the medications they wouldn't fuck his mind up so much he concluded.

"Are you going to try it again?" Bobby said turning back over his shoulder.

"Never," Cal said.

"That's the answer I'm looking for," Bobby said coming back and giving his brother a hug.

When Bobby left, Cal had time to reflect and to think about life thus far. He knew he had to change some things. He realized his drinking and drug problems were an issue. Medications, pot and occasional hard drugs were a frequent habit. He also knew he had a problem with womanizing and brawling. Cal had a lot of things to do to clean up his life.

His near death episode had opened his eyes and made him realize that life was worth living. He thought to himself, maybe he would get a new profession.

He laughed at himself after for just being fired from his last job. Bernie the patient there came up beside Cal.

"He won't stop you know" Bernie stammered, about something.

Cal tried to ignore him and shut him out. But, the more he did the more Bernie went on.

"He won't stop, he's going to do it some more" Bernie stuttered, he was going on about somebody.

"He's going to do what?" Cal asked.

"He's going to kill some more girls," Bernie said referring to Cal's dream.

Cal sat stunned at by what the man was saying. He was speechless when an elderly nurse came over to him.

He began to shake, his hands trembling, and the visions of his dreams coming out here in broad daylight.

"Mr. Rushton, is everything alright" she asked touching him on the shoulder.

Cal jumped "Shit!" he said out loud.

"Did I startle you?" she apologized.

"A bit," Cal said feeling the blood course through his veins, his heart pumping with excitement.

He got a sharp pain in the top of his head, wincing in pain. The pain was uncontrollable, gripping and antagonizing.

"Are you okay?" the nurse asked seeing his obvious discomfort.

"Just a bit faint," Cal replied, feeling light headed and woozy.

"I think you should lie down for a bit," the nurse said thinking the day had been too much for him.

The nurse put here hand on his arm "Is that okay," she said, trying to approach him slowly as to not startle him again.

"I'm al right" Cal scowled, the nurse was being to damn nice treating him like a child.

"Calm down Mr. Rushton" she urged, hearing the tone in his voice rise.

Cal felt more intense, a rush of adrenaline and intense pain in his head and shoulders. His arms were tingling for some reason. He didn't like this feeling, damn medications, he thought to himself again.

"Orderly," the nurse waved over the big orderly to come over and help.

The big man came over, his tall frame looming over Cal. His head looked small for his massive body. Can you assist Mr. Ruston to his room" the nurse knew he was extremely agitated for some reason. That was the last thing Cal remembered. He vaguely remembered the man touching him when he passed out. The next thing he knew he woke back up in bed. He didn't remember being wheeled back into his room or lifted back in bed.

A nurse was in his room checking on him.

"Sorry," the nurse apologized picking up something that had fallen to the floor.

"What happened?" Cal asked referring to the incident in the lobby.

"You fainted, probably exhaustion," the nurse explained.

"I feel a bit funny," Cal confessed, "My skin feels like pins and needles.

"It's probably the medication," the nurse said trying to ease his mind.

The nurse moved closer putting her back of her hand on his forehead. He looked at her his head still reeling from the headache and pain.

"You do feel a bit clammy," she told him.

The nurse smiled picking up a thermometer placing it in his mouth. He couldn't help look at her and how sweet she was to him.

Cal read her nametag on the crisp white uniform. Janice, a nice name he thought to himself, suddenly feeling at ease. Cal looked at her hands for a wedding band. The nurse noticed him looking at her hands. She knew what he was doing, she had been a nurse long enough to know when she was being checked out.

"Were not allowed to wear jewelry on this job," she smirked.

Cal didn't respond the thermometer still in his mouth, but he did feel a bit embarrassed that she had noticed.

"Normal," she said taking it out.

Cal waited for the nurse to leave before finally drifting off to sleep. Cal had a very strange dream. This time he wasn't falling, he found himself filling his car with gas at a service station. An attendant came out, a tall skinny man. The unshaven man wiped grease off his hands on a rag. He stood there smiling and friendly. He looked to be in his mid thirties and there was nothing out of place about the man.

"Check your oil?" he asked putting the greasy cloth on the bonnet of Cal's 71' Camaro.

Cal could feel the anger inside him growing; the man looked straight at him. His piercing eyes questioning Cal. The man quickly rubbed the grease off the hood, opening the hood of the car.

"Sorry," he said apologizing.

Cal's anger dissipated, he replaced the nozzle in the gas pump, screwing the gas cap on. Cal watched the man closely he seemed vaguely familiar from somewhere, but where?

Did he know him from one of his jobs, from around town, he couldn't figure it out in the dream and it was bothering him.

"She's good on oil," the attendant said lowering the hood.

"She sure is a beauty," the man said with a broad smile.

Cal went to pay the man for the gas, their hands met. Suddenly, his dream turned very violent.

He pictured flashes of a murder. A young woman was being brutally raped and strangled. They were in a car and she was fighting for her life. Her fingernails scratched at the window of the car. A look of terror in her eyes as her life was being snuffed out. Then another flash of a woman in some abandoned building being tortured and raped.

Cal took a step back feeling the terror of the women. A name flashed in Cal's head as the attendant turned to go back inside. Barker the last name on the tag on the overhauls said. It stuck out at him the name burning into his mind.

He woke shaky and startled by the dream. He woke up mumbling the name Barker. Over and over again he could see his face as well as the woman in the car. The nurse was standing there over his beside. She realized by looking at him that he was in distress, beads of sweat formed on his forehead.

"Bad dream Mr. Rushton," she asked seeing beads of sweat on his head.

"Horrible," he muttered, visualizing over and over.

"It's probably just the medication," she said referring to the pills on the tray.

Over the next couple of days Cal got his strength back. He had nightmares upon nightmares that he couldn't explain. Over and over the face of Barker, with the initials CR on it now in his dreams, each time there was a bit more to the name and a bit more vivid in memory. He woke up in a sweat again and again his head was splitting.

He couldn't understand the dream he was having; perhaps he needed psychiatric help in unraveling his dream. He didn't want to be evaluated again that would only mean more tests and more doctors. As it was he was being grilled over and over again, never did he mention the dreams or faces.

The next few days went by slowly, he was excited about the prospect of leaving the hospital. The only reason they were keeping him now was because of his headaches. If he said more they would only keep him longer and he didn't want that or need it, all he wanted was to get out and have a fresh start at life.

Bobby came into his room "How you doing Bro," he asked Cal.

"Ready to get the fuck out of here" Cal swore tiring of the whole situation.

"Got some good news for you then," Bobby said his eyes lighting up.

"What's that?" Cal waiting patiently for Bobby to tell him, he could go home.

"Got you a new job at a car dealership in town," Bobby told him, waiting for his response.

"Great perks, new car to drive, bonuses etc. if you do good," Bobby paused, "You'll do great, good way to meet new people."

"I just want to get out of here," Cal said hoping Bobby had news of his leaving, the disappointment showing on his face.

The doctor came into the room "How you feeling?" the doctor asked bending down looking into his eyes, "How's the headaches."

He held up Cal's chart, "Ready to join society again?" he asked looking over his bifocals at Cal.

"Hell yeah," Cal said excitedly, hearing the news he wanted to hear.

"No more foolishness," the doctor warned "Or we won't be letting you out next time."

"No doc, I've learned my lesson" Cal told him, the genuine tone showing in his voice.

"Okay then get your stuff ready," the doctor said looking at Bobby.

Cal and Bobby drove out of the parking lot in Bobby's truck. Bobby cranked the stereo as they got in. The sudden music startled Cal. It was great to feel the fresh air and see the outside world again. He promised himself he would never let anything like this happen again.

"Easy," Bobby said turning the volume down, noticing Cal's irritation.

"Guess I can't take sudden noises anymore," Cal said relaxing in the seat.

Cal and Bobby drove off making small talk concerning Cal's new life. Bobby drove into a different part of town. He turned into an apartment building complex turning off the engine.

"What's this place?" Cal asked confused, looking at the outside of the building.

"Your new home," Bobby smiled, and pleased that they had got him out of his last rat's nest.

"Heaven's Gate," Cal burst out laughing at the name of the apartment complex.

"Figured you needed a change of atmosphere," Bobby said shutting the truck off.

The two entered the building, going to the sixth floor, apartment 6. Cal looked at the hallway and laughed again. Thinking it was so funny that he was in Heaven's Gate, Sixth Floor, and Apartment 6.

"Is this a joke?" Cal said to Bobby who inserted the key into the apartment door.

"Kind of ironic isn't it," Bobby said opening the door.

Inside the apartment was clean and spacious. The ratty furniture didn't look all that bad in the new place. There were also a few new pieces of furniture that Cal never had. He looked around, the place smelled fresh and clean. Everything was like brand new even his crappy furniture looked decent.

There was definitely a woman's touch to the place. Bobby's wife Anne came out of the bedroom followed by Cal's sister Martha.

"Surprise," they shouted, both smiles on their faces and blowing on a kazoo.

"Marty," Cal smiled hugging his sister; it had been a long time since he had seen her.

The two embraced staring at each other. He looked her up and down, hugging her again. Tears welled up in his eyes, to think she had come all this way for him.

"You've lost weight," Marty said looking at Cal and pinching his stomach.

Supper was cooking in the kitchen, a new table, decorated with candles and flowers adorned the dining area.

Cal felt very comfortable in this new place. He actually felt at peace here. He was amazed that this place was his. This was the fresh start that he needed. The others could all tell that he was both amazed and happy with his new surroundings. The four sat down at the table to eat their supper. They conversed back and forth laughing and enjoying each other's company. It felt good to have the company and to feel that this was his new life.

"How did you manage all this?" Cal asked looking around at the surroundings.

"We all chipped in," Marty said "I hope you like it".

"I really don't know how to pay you back" Cal said tears in his eyes.

"You already have," Marty continued, "You were there when I needed you before.

"It really is great, but I can't afford the rent in a place like this," Cal said worried about the bills.

"Honey don't worry about the rent, Ben's taken care of that," she said referring to her husband.

Ben was quite well off and always got along with Cal. His offer to help Cal with a new start was from the heart.

"Ben has paid a years lease for you to get caught up," Marty said taking his hand in hers.

The four finished supper. Marty and Anne did the dishes while Cal and Bobby sat in the living room talking. He leaned back on the sofa looking at the clean well-kept place. He would make sure this place kept clean and tidy, he thought to himself. Bobby and Cal sat sipping coffee, and then Anne and Marty joined them.

Soon Bobby and Anne had to get home to their kids the baby sitter was waiting. Marty stayed behind wanting to spend sometime with her brother." How are you feeling?" Marty finally asked him, noticing the tired look in his eyes.

"Kind of strange, but fine considering I guess," he told her trying to explain something was wrong without coming right out with it.

"Any weird dreams or anything?" Marty asked, guessing right on the money that he was having dreams.

"Yes, how did you know," he paused "Nightmares, really horrible nightmares," Cal told her confessing.

"I went through the same thing," Marty confessed "After my incident."

"Were you clinically dead?" Cal asked prying for information to see if it was normal.

"Yes I saw the white light, that everyone claims to see when they die. I had the experience of extreme peace," she finished explaining her experience to him.

Cal sat listening to her story saying nothing. He wishes he saw a white light and not what he was seeing. How would he tell her about the dreams of pitch-black darkness? How would he tell her about the man's name blazed on his memory or the two dead women he had seen?

"What about you?" she asked finally.

"Can't remember anything," he lied "I wake up knowing I had a dream but can't remember them."

They talked some more, Marty left for her hotel room. She was going back to the hotel and then back home to her husband the next day.

After she left Cal thought about what she had seen, it was completely different than his visions. He wondered if what he was seeing was hell and what she was seeing was heaven. Cal was alone in his new home. He was thinking about all that had happened. For some strange reason thoughts of the patient at the institution came flooding in his mind. Bernie was telling him he was going to do it again. Was Bernie some kind of physic or something, or was it just mindless ramble on his part.

Cal lay down on the sofa and drifted off to sleep. He was in his nightmare world again of falling. Then just as suddenly Colin Ray Baker came into his head. The girl's face that was being murdered was clear. She was a classy well-dressed woman. Now he also saw the man's full name. She looked as though she came from money. She was at the gas pumps of the garage and the next thing he knew she was being brutally raped and killed. Cal's dream was more vivid this time, her beautiful blond hair soaked with blood. Her cries for help that no one answered. The foul contempt of the rapist, violating her body.

Cal couldn't believe this was happening, he felt helpless to help her. Cal wanted to help her but he couldn't. The victim screamed in agony, alone with the rapist to do, as he wanted. What was it he was seeing? Why did every dream have the same people and the same visions? Was he seeing something happening that really happened or was it just the medications he was taking? Cal was scared by the dreams and each one seemed worse.

CHAPTER II
STRANGE CLUES

He woke up sweating and his head was pounding out of control. He reached on the coffee table picking up the pill bottle. He sat up for a few minutes and turned the television set on. He sat there stunned by his latest dream and the full name of Colin Ray Barker, which he kept repeating in his mind.

The late news was on, without warning suddenly a face came on the screen. The news anchor announced the news.

"Missing person, if anyone has seen or heard from Kathleen Logan would they please contact the police immediately."

Cal froze on the sofa staring at her face, realizing that was the woman in his dreams. Why was she in his dreams what did this have to do with him. He sat for a long time spellbound by the vision of her face. She was dead that he knew by the dream he was having. Why was he seeing her, was she coming to him to tell him about it. Was there some kind of Physic Phenomenon that he didn't understand?

He got a massive headache thinking about the woman and the vision on the TV. He was sure she was the same woman. Morning was coming and the night turned to day. Cal had to find out more; he stayed on the sofa fixated on the TV. He kept watching the news over and over. Trying to figure out what was going on in his life.

Finally, he got dressed and went out into the chilly morning for some air. He walked for quite a distance when he saw the convenience store. He went inside and picked up the local paper. The picture on the cover glared at him.

"Well Known politicians daughter missing." Cal was stunned by her picture he couldn't believe what was happening. He took the newspaper back home with him. Sitting on the sofa he got out scissors and carefully cut the picture out of the paper. He read the story over and over trying to find some kind of clue. He put the pictures on the coffee table looking at them carefully, closing his eyes. Nothing happened he didn't have any strange visions.

He closed his eyes again drifting off to sleep. His dream came back again, the smile of Colin Ray Barker haunting his dream. He had a vision of Kathleen Logan screaming for help. She was there again, asking and pleading for help. No one was there to help her, why was he still seeing this dead woman. He woke up this time with a strange feeling.

He picked up the picture on the coffee table in front of him. He could see her lying in an old building of some kind but it wasn't clear. A chill ran down his spine at the visions he was seeing, but why him?

Cal thought it must have something to do with his near death experience, but what? It was now noon and he hadn't eaten since the night before. A knock came on the door startling him. He answered the door to his brother's smiling face. Cal was surprised by his early visit. He must have stopped by on his way to work.

"How you doing today?" Bobby asked him, noticing he looked like he hadn't slept at all.

"Checking up on me are you?" Cal said letting him in.

"Well that to but I thought we might do lunch together" he said "My treat".

He wanted to tell Bobby about all the strange events, but wasn't sure he would understand. He might want to take him to a doctor and have it checked out. He didn't want Bobby or anyone else thinking he was crazy. He had to figure this out himself and there had to be some kind of logical explanation to what was happening, but what?

"Thanks, maybe some other time" Cal said as Bobby sat down on the sofa.

"Got a few things to take care of" he said referring to his visions and the articles in the papers.

Bobby picked up the newspaper, noticing the picture and article cut out. One of the pictures of Kathleen Logan fell onto the floor. He had a stunned look on his face wondering what it meant.

"What's this?" Bobby said curiously.

Cal had no choice but to confess to Bobby. He told him what had been happening. Bobby sat and listened, not interrupting Cal, letting him finish. He didn't want to say anything until Cal was done explaining, but it sounded pretty damn strange to him.

"That's pretty fucked up," Bobby said looking at him with a weird expression.

"I heard about that girl, her father's a big wig lawyer and politician" Bobby told him.

"Yeah, but I don't know what to do, I can't figure this out" Cal confessed, thinking about what was happening to him.

"I don't know whether to shit or go blind," Cal said referring to an old saying.

"I would say shit" Bobby said "Look Cal it's probably the pills and the trauma you've been through" he continued "You probably fell asleep with the news on and then had the wild dream. Plus, you've probably got withdrawal from drugs and booze" Bobby finished, making excuses for something he couldn't explain.

Cal agreed picking up the newspaper and pictures rolling them into a ball. He took them to the trashcan throwing them in. He wasn't convinced but it made more sense than what he was going through.

"What about lunch now?" Bobby asked again.

Cal was about to say something when he noticed the paper hanging on the fridge. He didn't remember the paper there last night when he went to bed. Where did that piece of paper come from, he was thinking going to the fridge to look at it. At first he thought it was probably a note from Marty, until he looked at it more.

"Help me please" was scrawled in black ink hanging from a fridge magnet.

"Think I'll pass, didn't get much sleep" Cal said a chill going down his spine, realizing this thing whatever was had more too it than he could explain.

Bobby left shortly after; telling Cal not to worry his nightmares would go away. Cal got changed into some clean jeans a clean shirt. He couldn't remember the last time he ironed a shirt. He was amused at the smallest things that he had overlooked before. He rubbed his chin in thought. Noticing the thick stubble of hair on his face. He looked in the mirror at himself. He shaved, brushed his teeth and combed his hair. He ran his hands through his hair, thinking he really needed a haircut. He thought about it if he was starting a new life he had to look like a new man, and act like one too.

"This won't do," he said out loud referring to his hair.

Finally, satisfied with his appearance he left the apartment closing the door behind him.

He thought as he entered the parking lot about his change in attitude. He never gave much thought about what people thought about him before. He got into his 71' Camaro, disgusted by the mess the car was in. The acrid smell of cigarette butts wrappers and ashes cluttered the car. He started the car, taking out a pack of cigarettes from the dash of his car. Without thinking he looked at them opening the glove box back open and throwing them in. He felt like an entirely new person. He knew what he had to do next.

He had to find out more about the disappearance of Kathleen Logan. As well he had to find out if Colin Ray Barker existed. He still had doubts in his mind about the whole ordeal. But, if he could find peace of mind he had to do something. The proper place to start would be look in the telephone book. Maybe, he could find out where Kathleen Logan or Colin Ray Barker resided. He sat in the parking lot letting his car warm up.

He started cleaning the mess in his car. He reached into the backseat, seeing a plastic bag he could use to put the garbage in. The bag wasn't empty; it felt heavy like there was something in it. He pulled it up onto his lap and opening the bag.

"What the fuck!" he said reaching in the bag.

He pulled out a wad of money, all in 100-dollar bills. Four bundles of 100-dollar bills each wrapped in an elastic band. In the bottom of the bag there was a note. Where did this money come from and why was it here? Cal was confused; the car was locked and had been used since his stay in the hospital.

"Guess who?" was scribbled on the note.

Cal felt the blood drain from his face. Who would put this kind of money in his car? Who would have access to his car? Why, would they give him this kind of money? He quickly shoved the money back into the bag, looking outside the car feeling very nervous.

He could see nothing; nobody appeared to be watching him. How much was there he wondered? Whatever, the reason it took his mind off his other dilemma. He sat in the car for a minute looking outside to see if anyone was near watching him. He opened the car door stepping outside into the coolness of the morning and looking around some more. He could see no one; he shook his head confused by what was happening.

He took the bag back inside his apartment to count it and hide it. His hands shook nervously as he dumped the contents on the coffee table. He double-checked the door making sure it was locked. He took the band off one of the bundles and began counting. There were one hundred, 100-dollar bills in that one stack.

"Oh my God One hundred thousand dollars" he said out loud.

That means there was 300,000 dollars here. Who would have that kind of money, and even if they did why would they be giving it to him. Was he being framed? Was this just some kind of setup to frame him for the murder of Kathleen Logan? This was a weird situation he was in, strange and bizarre. Thoughts crossed his mind, what if he was being set up for something? What if someone made a mistake and the owner came looking for their money?

He didn't know what do to. He took the money and slipped it back into the bag, wrapping it tightly. He wandered around the apartment aimlessly looking for a place to hide the stash of money. He couldn't make his mind up on a safe place. Finally, he pulled the tray from under the refrigerator patting it down and sliding the tray back into place. Surely, the owners or owner would come back for the money.

Whoever it was knew which car they had put the money in and would eventually track him down. Should he tell anyone? Should he call Bobby? He racked his mind for someone who had that kind of money. He knew that Marty and husband Ben had money but not this kind of money. He had to figure out something to figure out where this money had come from. He stared at the note on the refrigerator.

The phone rang startling him. "Cal you watching the news" Bobby's voice sounded excited.

"No, why?" he said, clicking the television on.

"Turn it on WCTV, quick" Bobby's voice had a tone of urgency.

Cal clicked on the TV; there was a news conference about to start.

"Okay got it," Cal said sitting on the sofa, feeling anticipation.

The police chief was standing ready for the conference. Microphones, cameras and reporters surrounded the Police Chief. The type at the bottom of the screen flashed. News...updates... Live, Concerning the disappearance of Kathleen Logan.

Cal got a funny feeling in the pit of his stomach looking at the words and waiting for the Police Chief to start talking.

"The disappearance of Kathleen Logan has come to a tragic end," the Police chief stated.

Neither Bobby nor Cal spoke as they both watched the news.

"Early this morning at approximately six thirty am, the body of Kathleen Logan was found". "The police have no leads or suspects to make public at this time". "There has been three hundred thousand dollar reward offered to anyone that has information that may lead to the arrest and conviction of the person or persons involved".

Cameras flashed, reporters quickly started asking questions. The crowd of reporters worked in a frenzy of activity.

Cal watched unable to comprehend what he was seeing. What was going on, he had seen the death of Kathleen Logan, in his dreams and now it had come true.

"You still there?" Bobby asked Cal.

"I gotta go" Cal said hanging the phone up, suddenly feeling sick to his stomach.

The phone rang again. "Did you hear all that Cal?" Bobby said his voice astonished.

"Yeah, I don't know what to say?" Cal said stunned.

He mulled over telling Bobby about the money but dismissed the idea. If he told him it might put him and his family in danger. Thinking about the money it was the exact amount being offered for any information leading to the arrest or conviction for information for the murder of Kathleen Logan.

"What you said about her being dead, it's not a coincidence" Bobby said a note of concern in his voice; by the tone of his voice he knew that Cal was telling the truth.

"I don't know Bobby, maybe it was just a nightmare?" he suggested, trying to hide the idea that there was more too it than he wanted to believe himself.

"You have to find out when and where it happened Cal?" Bobby said trying to sound helpful.

"I just want to forget it Bobby" Cal said sounding mildly irritated.

"Cal I think we have to find out what happened" Bobby said calmly. "Something's strange here, she disappeared the same day you tried to kill yourself" Bobby said trying to figure things out.

"I'm coming over," Bobby said exasperated. Cal hung up the phone.

Cal was right he had to find out what was going on. He had to figure out what happened to Kathleen Logan. He still wasn't sure if Kathleen Logan and the money were related. Was it just a coincidence the money and her death or were they related to each other. The phone rang again. Cal was nervous from the amount of cash and the amount of the reward money.

"Just come over Bobby, for Christ sakes" Cal said thinking the voice on the other end was not Bobby.

"Is this Cal Rushton?" the female voice asked?

Cal apologized and asked who it was. Cal felt embarrassed that he had answered the phone in such a tone.

"This is county general hospital calling" she paused "Do you know an Eva Tucker?" she asked.

"Yes" he answered cautiously.

"Ms. Tucker is in intensive care and wants to see you," the nurse added.

"What happened?" Cal asked, the tone of his voice held concern for her well-being.

"You had better come over, she's in critical condition" the nurse continued.

"Okay, I'll be right over" Cal said clicking down the receiver, Cal went over in his mind as to what must have happened to Eva. Why would she be asking for him, after all she never visited him in the hospital, she never seemed to concerned about Cal at all in the past few months.

Cal called Bobby explaining about Eva and that she was asking for him at the hospital. Cal arrived at the hospital with his brother Bobby. It was 2:30pm when they arrived. The drive to the hospital was rough. A fresh snowfall had made the roads slippery in places. Inside the hospital, Cal found out which room Eva was in.

Cal talked to the nurse and asked her what had happened. She told Cal that Eva had been brutally attacked and raped. She went on to say that Eva had somehow managed to escape her attacker and was very courageous. Outside of Eva's door a police officer stood guard. Cal stopped at the door telling the officer who he was. The officer escorted him to Eva's bedside. Eva was fading in and out of consciousness.

The officer said that most of what she was saying didn't make sense. Her head was bandaged, her face beaten and swollen. Her eyes were swollen shut to the extent the doctors feared she would lose the sight of her left eye. As Cal touched her hand a wave of pain and anger engulfed him. The picture in his mind of her being brutally assaulted and raped was vivid. The man face was not evident, but he thought of Colin Ray Barker. The man's hands were around her throat as he beat and raped her. The more she struggled the more intense it became. Finally, a knife was pulled; he loped off her right ear.

The look of terror in her eyes showed the terror she was feeling. Cal let go of her hand in a jolt of reality. Why was he seeing these visions, did the near death incident he had give him some kind of powers to see these things? He looked down at her bandaged face, wondering why this was all happening to him. There was some kind of connection to his visions and what was going on within his dreams and mind. Now he had the power to touch someone and see what was happening to him or her.

"Cal, is that you" she muttered groggily, her voice weak and whispered.

"Yes do you know who did this?" Cal asked hoping she might be able to give him some kind of clue.

"No, he came to my house, posing as the telephone repair man" she managed to say.

"He knows you Cal, he asked how you were before he attacked me," she said fading back into unconsciousness.

Cal was confused again the man that attacked her knew Cal. What the hell was going on here was this man in the dreams the same one that attacked Eva. He tried to scan his mind trying to think of who this might be.

"He knows me?" Cal said out loud his curiosity turning to anger and guilt.

The police officer stood listening to the conversation. "We need you to come down to headquarters" the officer told him "You might know something information to help us find this man".

"What for?" Cal asked the officer, taking his eyes off Eva and turning them to the officer.

"Just some questions we need to ask" the officer continued.

"You don't think I had anything to do with this do you?" Cal said his voice showing shock.

"Just routine Mr. Rushton, were just trying to shed some light on this attack" the officer responded.

The officer told him that a Detective Mundale would be waiting for him to come in. He also told him that if he didn't go voluntarily that he would be charged with, withholding information. Cal was curious to see what Mundale had to say.

He thought that Barker was the man behind the murder and assault of Eva Tucker. Cal also knew he had to be careful with what he had to say to the detective. He met Bobby in the waiting room, briefly explaining to him about Eva and the subsequent questioning. Cal stood for a minute staring back into the room where Eva Tucker was lying in critical condition.

They walked out of the hospital, Cal feeling in such a daze.

Bobby drove Cal to the police station; Bobby took a seat in the waiting room. Cal introduced himself at the front desk. The officer on duty escorted Cal into Lieutenant Jim Mundale's office. Inside Mundale sat behind his desk looking at paperwork. His desk was cluttered with papers; the Lieutenant didn't look up from the papers in front of him at first ignoring Cal.

"Mr. Rushton to see you detective" the officer told him.

"Thanks Mitch" Mundale said looking up at Cal.

"Please take a seat Mr. Rushton" Mundale replied, sliding some of his papers to the side of the desk.

Mundale was a stocky well-built man. He didn't look the part of a law enforcement office. He was a younger man in his late twenties to early thirties, Cal thought. He looked to young to be a Lieutenant, but not to young for doing this type of work. Mundale looked up again taking his glasses off. He had a bushy mustache and deep blue penetrating eyes. Cal plunked down in the chair in front of Mundale's cluttered desk. He felt nervous and didn't like the feel of the office.

"Mr. Rushton, I've been reading over a file on you" he paused flipping the

Page. "You've had a few brushes with the law," he continued, turning another page.

Cal sank in silence, wondering why he was being picked apart. Was he a suspect in Eva Tucker's assault?

"Drunk and disorderly, assault, verbal threats". "You've got quite a temper Mr. Rushton" Mundale said staring up at him.

"You don't think I honestly had anything to do with the assault on Eva, do you?" Cal countered waiting for Mundale to acknowledge why he was brought in for questioning.

"Mr. Rushton, or can I call you Cal" Mundale asked folding his hands on his desk and leaning forward across the desk.

"Am I under arrest?" Cal felt a wave of nervousness comes over him.

"No, but everyone is a suspect" Mundale went on "There's something here going on, this guy knows who you are".

"Then why the fuck would Eva want me to come to see her, if I was guilty"

Cal argued leaning forward getting into Mundales face.

"Your right Cal, However, sometimes the victim in such cases blame themselves for what happened". Mundale finished.

Cal sat there amazed by the Lieutenant's insinuations. He knew Mundale was grasping at straws and didn't have anything on him. Mundale was young to be a Lieutenant Cal thought. Mundale's chubby young face made him look like he was in his early twenties.

"Do you know anyone by the name of Frank?" Mundale asked.

"No, I'm sorry I don't" Cal said, sitting for a minute trying to recognize the name.

"Ms. Tucker had mentioned the name Frank" Mundale pointed out.

"It might have been just rambling on her part, were not sure" Mundale told him.

"So you think this Frank guy had something to do with Eva?" Cal asked him.

"He was posing as a telephone repair man, I thought maybe you knew someone by the name of Frank that had a grudge against you". Mundale said flipping another page.

Mundale went on to ask him a few more questions. Where he was last night, who was with him? He asked Cal to call him if he thought of anything.

After Cal left Mundale's office, he flipped open another file.

Inside the file were pictures of the murdered Kathleen Logan. The reports were similar to that of Eva Tucker's assault. It was the same method of strangulation, rape, brutal assault and the most bizarre the cutting off of the right ear. Mundale had not been able to gain much information from Eva Tucker.

Whoever had assaulted her might even try to finish the job. Mundale had an officer stationed at her hospital room in case the assailant tried to come back.

The Detective knew that Eva Tucker had escaped and was found on the back road of Fox Creek. Apparently, the man had broken into her home, abused, assaulted, raped her and left her there to die. He then must have taken her and dumped her on the side of the road for dead. Eva couldn't remember much about how she got where she did. Mundale thought about her, she was very fortunate to have survived such an ordeal.

The criminal usually makes sure the victim is dead in such vicious cases. He thought perhaps the criminal or criminals had let her live, as a message to the police department. There was no way he could tie up the lose ends. He did know that whoever had done the crime was driving a White Van. There were just too many questions unanswered.

Mundale was waiting for more information from the crime scene to try and piece the puzzle together. One thing Mundale was sure of was that whoever assaulted Eva Tucker was the same man that had killed Kathleen Logan. There were just to many of the same techniques and the cutting off as the right ear. Was that some kind of bizarre trophy for the murderer? Somewhere in this mystery the clue led to Cal Rushton. The criminal had identified him to Eva Tucker.

Cal drove home with Bobby. Bobby asked him what was going on, wondering what had happened to Eva and why he was considered a suspect. Cal told him that the police just wanted to ask him some questions about the assault of Eva. Cal never mentioned Kathleen Logan; his mind was on the attack of Eva Tucker. The strange coincidence of Kathleen Logan and now Eva Tucker made him think that the two were connected. Would he start seeing Eva in his dreams and visions? He thought back to the severe beating that they both had, it all seemed so similar. But, still the thing remained whoever was doing this knew about him and somehow knew where he lived. It was as though they could see what was going on in his mind.

They drove into the yard of Cal's apartment building complex, Cal told Bobby he needed to rest. The storm had subsided for now. Cal's 71' Camaro was buried with snow. Cal elected to travel with Bobby in his four-wheel drive, rather than take the chance with his car.

Cal went inside the apartment building as Bobby drove off. Cal unlocked the door of his apartment, making sure to re-lock and proceeded to the stash of money hidden under the refrigerator. He slid out the tray from under the fridge and stared into the plastic bag. All the strange events of the past week had left him mentally exhausted. The strangest thing was the note and huge sum of money, which was the exact amount offered as a reward. He was weary sliding the tray back into place.

His mind turned to Colin Ray Barker. Was the money, Barker and his near death experience in some way related? He sat on the sofa drifting off to sleep.

His dream started at a peaceful pace. He was walking in a meadow full of wild flowers. The white fluffy clouds above floated dreamily. Butterflies fluttered across the meadow. A babbling brook ran winding its way gracefully to another journey.

Cal sat with a picnic basket, a woman wearing white stood back to him. The woman's long blonde hair was glistening in the sun. She was picking a daisy and saying. "He loves me, he loves me not". He could see the pedals of the flower twirling in the air as they made their way to the ground. Cal lay back on the blanket feeling the serene peace. The sun beaming through the clouds suddenly turned angry and gray. He sat up looking at the woman. She turned around her clothing dripping with blood. Her face was full of tears; it was the face of Kathleen Logan.

"Help me please," she begged tears flowing down her cheeks.

Cal was startled out of his dream. His heart raced, his head hurt, perspiration covered his face. The nightmare made Cal even more positive that the first thing to do was find Kathleen Logan's home. Talk with her father and mother if need be. He had to clear his conscious to rid himself of the horrible dream. The one thing that remained constant in his dreams was constant thought of Colin Ray Barker. He was positive that Colin Ray Barker was the murderer.

The nightmares continued for Cal later on that night. Cal now dreaded sleep, always being haunted by either Kathleen Logan's face or the pitch black hole he was falling into. During the night Cal awoke twice the first nightmare was the pitch black hole again and the feeling of falling. The second dream was Kathleen Logan, this time she was standing facing him with flowers in her arms. She was crying and asked why he wouldn't help her. Colin Ray Barker came up beside her and smiled.

"What's wrong Cal don't have the guts?" Barker stood and laughed, taunting him.

Cal woke up at 5am and decided he had to come up with some kind of plan. He knew if he went to his doctor and asked why he was having these dreams, the doctor would just blame it on the medications he was taking. He didn't want to end up back on some phys ward. He had to find the answers himself, once and for all.

He carefully got the money out of its hiding place. He unbundled the bills; maybe there was a clue in there somewhere. He plugged the coffee percolator on and went to the kitchen drawer. He reached in the drawer and pulled out a pack of cigarettes. He searched for a lighter but found none. Finally, he found a book of matches. On the booklet of matches was the name of a downtown bar. The bar was a dive called the Rusty Bumper. Funny he had seen it but hadn't been in that dump for years. He wondered to himself opening up the matches and striking one. He nearly burnt his fingers when he saw the name of the phone number. Kathleen 555-1751.

"Fuck" he said staring at the phone number.

CHAPTER III
VISIONS

Cal had no idea whose matches they were but they weren't his. He decided to call the phone number on the matches. It was now 6am; he'd probably wake someone if he called. But, he had to know if the number was legitimate or not. A tired female voice answered on the fourth ring.

"Hello" the sleepy voice said.

"I probably have the wrong number. Is Kathleen there" he asked.

"Who is this?" the voice suddenly awake, alert and curious.

"An old acquaintance of hers in town for a few days" Cal lied, noticing the concern on the other end of the phone.

"Kathleen died," she said exasperated.

"What?" Cal said trying to sound shocked and upset.

"Who is this?" she asked again trying to get information out of him.

"Colin" Cal said the first name popping in his head.

Cal apologized for calling telling her how sorry he was to hear the bad news. He told her that he hadn't been around for a few years and was just looking up some old friends. He lied trying to make up a story on the spot.

"My name is Amanda," she told him finally "I was Kathleen's roommate".

"I'm sorry once again Amanda, is there anything I can do?" Cal asked a hint of sympathy in his voice.

Amanda found him interesting and wanted to know more about how he knew her. Cal suggested they get together for coffee and he would come pick her up. She told him that would be fine and they set a time for 11:00am. Cal hung up the phone after getting her address for a coffee shop downtown, which she supplied He was hoping maybe to get a look at the apartment and maybe a clue. Maybe he could get a lead on Colin Ray Barker.

Cal got showered and cleaned up and sat down at the coffee table counting out some money.

"All this money" he muttered counting out the bills.

Where did it come from he thought again? He had lots of confusing issues to contend with. He came to the last pile of bills, halfway through it something stuck out. One of the bills had something written on it.

"Bus depot—1 pkg."

What was this strange and bizarre message? Did this mean there was a package for him at the bus depot?

Cal left to meet Amanda at the coffee shop. He didn't know what to expect from the meeting. He was hoping she would shed some light on the mystery. However, he was also concerned she might start asking questions he couldn't answer. He knew nothing about Kathleen Logan's history. He didn't know what school she attended where she grew up nothing.

Cal decided he would go to the library to do some studying on the matter. At the library he sat in front of the computer reading the headlines of the murder. There he gathered information on Kathleen Logan, where she studied, where she grew up. Most of it was online; all you have to do is search by name.

He also studied the obituary column again to familiarize himself with her family. He then decided he would wait to go the bus depot after he had his meeting with Amanda. He knew he would have to make up some bogus story about Kathleen, but what? He knew very little about Kathleen or even her family.

Maybe this was a mistake he thought to himself entering the small café. He looked around the small café, looking for a woman that might be Amanda. However there were no women in the café that fit her age. Maybe she's late he told himself. He decided to sit at the counter. A dozen red and white stools stood lined up against the counter. He sat at the very end of the counter making sure there was enough room between him and the other customers.

He took his seat; a pretty dark haired waitress came over to wait on him. He sat waiting patiently for her; nervous that he was doing the wrong thing, but at the same time doing something he knew he had to do.

"May I help you sir?" she asked politely looking at him.

"A coffee please, black, one sugar" he asked.

"Are you waiting for someone sir?" she asked returning with the coffee.

"Yes" he answered, trying not to be too obvious.

"You must be Colin" the waitress responded smiling at him.

"I'm Amanda," the waitress told him.

"Oh, pleased to meet you" Cal said extending his hand.

She accepted his handshake and looked at him confused. "Denise would you cover for me?" she asked one of the other waitresses.

"I didn't realize you worked here," Cal said as the other woman came from out back.

"Well sort of" she said turning his mug around to the logo.

Amanda's in bright red lettering explained to Cal what she meant.

"You're the owner then" Cal smiled.

"Yes" she went on "Should I know you?" she asked.

"I doubt it, I grew up in Mansfield, Kathleen's families hometown" Cal lied remembering the article he had read about Senator Logan.

"Oh I see" her eyes squinted a bit.

"I was going to say, I've know Kathleen since High School and she's never mentioned the name Colin to me" she said waiting for his response.

"As I said it's been a long time" Cal said realizing he was being cornered by her.

"Then you must have know Kathleen's brother, Peter," she said testing him.

"You mean Michael Junior," he said remembering the article again.

"Yes, I meant Michael" she corrected herself; she was testing him to make sure of who he said he was.

"We played together as children" Cal said, trying to come up with something.

"Look I don't know who you are, or what you want. But, if you don't leave now I'll have to call the police" She said her voice turning harsh "unless of course you are the police, and I already answered enough of their questions".

"Please give me a chance to explain myself," Cal asked, realizing he had been caught in his lie.

47

"This had better be damn good" she replied taking off her apron, her anger very evident.

"I can't tell you this in here" Cal said lowering his voice so the other customers couldn't hear him.

"Are you a reporter, a cop what?" Amanda demanded, unsure of what he was talking about or what he wanted from her.

"None of those, it's really hard to explain," he told her trying to convince her he was harmless.

"Look I don't know who you are, I'm not about to trust you," she said her tone toning down, as to not disturb the other customers.

"All I know is Kathleen has been asking me to help her" Cal began.

"What the hell does that mean?" Amanda said her voice rising again, she could feel her anger rising, this man was some kind of joke, she told herself.

"Everything okay?" one of the customers asked from down the counter.

"It's okay Bill," she said referring to the big man.

"I told you it's hard to explain, but I can't tell you here" he insisted, his voice lowering.

"Well you had better try" she said sternly her eyes wavering towards the big man. It was a friendly warning that if he didn't start explaining she would tell the big man that he was giving her problems.

"I had a near death experience, since then Kathleen has haunted my dreams". He whispered, pulling back his collar enough to show the red mark around his neck.

How was he going to explain this to her? She would never believe such a lame story, but it was the truth and that's all he had to go on.

"I know you don't understand" he paused "the truth is neither do I" he confessed. "But, all I know is Kathleen Logan's death haunts me everyday". "I see visions of her and what happened, I'm trying to figure out who her killer was" he finished, taking the coffee cup and cupping it between his hands.

She stared at the now faint red mark around his neck. Amanda Riley, was speechless, she listened intently. Not sure whether to take him seriously or not. Whatever it was about him she wasn't sure, but oddly enough she believed him. She wanted to here the rest of the story to see if he was a lunatic or someone that honestly believed in what he was saying.

"I was hoping you might be able to help me," he told her.

"I'm not sure how you can but Kathleen is haunting me" he ended waiting, a look of desperation evident on his face.

"Wait here a minute" she told him stepping away from the counter and going out the back door to the kitchen. He sat waiting, staring around the small, quaint café. It was a dimly lit, quiet almost serene setting. Under other circumstances it would have been a nice place to come. It had a friendly warm feeling to it. The well-decorated café was clean, aromatic and romantic. It was a place to bring someone for a quiet lunch or a business meeting.

Amanda Riley came back wearing her jacket when she returned. He looked at her standing beside him, not knowing what else to say.

"Are you ready?" she asked him coming from behind the lunch counter.

"Sure" Cal said taking his wallet out to pay for the coffee.

"Don't worry about that" she insisted

Cal followed her outside, surprised that she had agreed at all to go with him alone.

The winter still held a defiant chill in the air. People were hustling and bustling up and down the main street. Most people were in a hurry to get out of the frigid climate. The small city was a business city. There weren't any huge sky scrappers, looming above the sky. It was a town depending on its seaport for shipping and small factories to keep it alive. The gray sky above told of maybe another snowstorm.

Cal looked at the sky now wondering which steps he would have to take to figure out what was going on.

"Where's your car?" she asked waiting for his reply.

"I always take the bus in the winter, I hate winter driving". She said, indicating the slippery new snowfall still on the sidewalks.

They got to Cal's 71' Camaro and headed down the street. Cal remembered the bus depot and the package that was there. Should he stop and pick it up, he mulled it over in his mind. He had to know what else was waiting there for him. What would the next clue to this bizarre nightmare be?

"Do you mind if I make a quick stop?" Cal asked looking over at her, noticing how pretty she was with her hair down.

Amanda had long brown hair, which was down now. Her big brown eyes and beautiful smile, very pretty face, but her long hair made her that more attractive to him. She turned to look at him, her dark brown eyes making contact with his.

"Whatever, as long as it's quick, I have to be back in a couple hours," she told him.

Cal pulled into the bus depot. He entered the old bus terminal, which was full of people waiting for buses. Cal walked to the wicket, a frail looking elderly man waited on him. Cal wasn't sure if the package would be in his name or someone else's name.

"Can I help you sir?" the man asking putting down his pen from his paperwork.

"Yes, I believe you have a package for me, Cal Rushton" he said putting his hands on the counter.

The little man returned to the counter carrying a small box wrapped in brown paper. He got out a pen and paper for Cal to sign for the package. His gnarled hands handing the pen to Cal to sign for.

"Been here a couple days or so now" the man waiting for Cal to sign for the package.

"What do I owe you for this?" Cal asked him, looking up at Cal from the paper.

"Just show me some identification and it's yours" the old man responded.

Cal pulled out his wallet showing the man his driver's license. The man slides the box over to Cal. He was curious the old man seemed to have a good memory; he wondered if he might remember the person that dropped the package off.

"By the way, do you happen to remember who dropped this package off"?

Cal asked hoping for a clue.

"Strange thing about this package, it was just left on the counter with an envelope attached" the old man nodded.

"The envelope had a twenty dollar bill inside and a note," he added.

"Do you still have the note?" Cal asked, curious to compare it with any other writing samples he might have of the stranger.

"No sorry sir, long gone" the old man said picking up his pen again beginning to scribble on his paperwork.

Cal went back out to the car where Amanda was waiting. He put the package in the back seat. He was wondering who knew his name and who would have left the package for him. The whole mystery seemed a bit un-nerving. He felt as if he was being watched at all times and someone knew his whereabouts everything about him.

"More mystery" Cal muttered out loud.

"Pardon" Amanda asked, curious about the strange looking package he was carrying.

"I'll explain later" Cal told her, looking at the package in the backseat and wondering what was in it.

"Where too?" Cal asked looking over at Amanda. She had touched up her makeup while waiting for Cal. She was even more beautiful now, if that was possible. She didn't look the least bit threatened by Cal, it was more curious about him than anything.

"My place she said, 174 O'Brien Street" she said not hesitating.

"I guess you trust me anyways," Cal said turning to her, turning the car and heading for her home.

"I guess, do I call you Colin or is that even your name?" she asked, finally.

The car sped back down main street "No it's Cal Rushton" he said holding his hand out to her as a gesture of a handshake.

"Mr. Rushton you are a bit of a mystery aren't you?" she snickered accepting his hand.

The woman Cal thought is very brave and clever as well. She might be able to help him unravel a clue to the mystery he thought.

"I'm sorry I hope I can explain on the way to your place," He said pulling up to a red light.

"Please do" she insisted, waiting for his explanation.

Cal explained about his near death experience and his dreams. He left out the black hole he was falling into and the money he had found in the car. He told her about Kathleen and Colin Ray Barker. She sat listening to him trying to grasp the things Cal was telling her. He told her the package in the backseat was something else, another clue. Explaining that he wasn't sure what was in it, but he knew it was something to do with Kathleen Logan.

They pulled into the driveway of the small apartment building. The building looked quaint and clean on the outside. Suddenly, Cal had a weird vision of someone sitting in front of the building. He saw Kathleen Logan enter the building as if through the eyes of someone else. He sat in a daze getting a chill up his spine and his head began to pound.

"Are you okay?" Amanda asked noticing his distress.

Cal told her about the vision he had, followed usually by a headache.

"That's another reason I believe you, I have a strange belief in you," she told him reaching out and touching his arm.

Cal felt calm when her hand touched his arm.

Inside the building was clean and well lit. Security was not an issue in this building. If someone forgot their keys all they had to do was buzz another tenant in from the entrance. The small building was four stories with 6 apartments on each floor.

"Everyone knows everyone in this building," she told him turning the key in the fourth floor apartment.

The apartment was well decorated, clean and colorful. It was easy to tell that two women lived in the apartment. It was kept neat and tidy, everything had a place to be stored.

"Nice place" Cal said looking at the surroundings.

The patio had a nice deck over looking the street below. The apartment was in the front of the building, so it was easy to see coming and going. Amanda showed Cal around the main rooms before entering Amanda's bedroom.

Then they went into Kathleen's room. Furniture and her clothing were still there in the place she had left them. Some dirty clothes were scattered on the floor here and there. She must have been busy or was she always a bit of a slob in her own room, Cal wondered.

"Excuse the mess, Kathleen was a bit of a slob, but the police didn't help matters any either," she said scooping down and gathering the dirty laundry.

"The only people that have been in here since her disappearance were the police" she told him.

"This is the first time for me to come in here since" she paused tears welling up in her eyes. "I've been staying with friends closer to work as to not remind of Kathleen" she said looking at her clothing.

"Do you mind?" Cal said looking at the picture on the nightstand.

"No please" she encouraged him.

Cal went over to the nightstand picking up the picture. The picture was of Kathleen at some kind of Christmas party. He got a strange vision of her in this bedroom. She was laughing and sprawled out on the bed.

He suddenly felt like he was watching her the night of her disappearance.

"Don't you show anyone these?" she teased as the flash bulb went off. Then he pictured her body in the warehouse dead. Cal felt a wave of darkness come over him, his knees buckling under him. Amanda noticed his distress and grabbed his arm. The vision was powerful and without warning. First he had a vision of her here in this room and then dead on the warehouse floor.

"Oh my God, are you alright?" she said trying to help him from falling over.

Cobwebs filled his brain momentarily. He felt weak and woozy and thought for a minute he was going to throw up.

"Give me a second" He said sitting down on the edge of Kathleen's bed.

"What did you see?" she asked helping him to sit down.

Amanda squatted down in front of him her hands taking hold of his shaking hands.

"He was here," Cal said groggily, referring to the killer.

"What, who was here?" she said shocked by the comment.

"The killer" Cal said as he felt Amanda's hand touch him again.

He calmed down his heart-stopped racing. He started to feel better the weakness was going away.

"He took pictures of her in the nude" Cal said shaking his head in disbelief.

"In this room?" Amanda shuttered.

"Yes Colin Ray Barker was here in this room" Cal hesitated not sure, there was no face only the name Colin Ray Barker bouncing around in his head.

"You're kidding," she said sitting down beside him on the bed.

Cal asked Amanda if she knew of Colin Ray Barker. Amanda told Cal that the name Colin didn't ring any bells.

"She had a problem with men," Amanda told him. "Men and booze and pills" Amanda went on. She went on to tell Cal that Kathleen never had a steady boyfriend for more than a couple months at a time. She had come close to getting married to a man a few years previous and found him cheating on her. After that she trusted no man and began to use men. Amanda had warned Kathleen that she was going to get hurt someday. Kathleen said she would never let another man hurt her again. Amanda offered her to move in and to help her pay her bills. It was an excuse to try and help Kathleen clean up her life. Amanda saw all the problems she was having and wanted to help her.

She said Kathleen seemed to be calming down a bit of her habits. She told Amanda that she had met someone that she liked. She said he was fairly wealthy and that she would marry for money not love. She had been seeing him a couple of weeks before she disappeared.

Cal sat listening intently, knowing fool well the man was most likely Colin Ray Barker. Whoever was taking pictures of Kathleen had her trust. Cal closed his eyes picturing Barker in his mind. He picked up the picture again. This time he didn't feel the rage and anger. He sat very calm, Amanda sitting beside him holding onto one of his hands.

Kathleen was drinking hard liquor. A man appeared next too her. He was standing back to; he was helping her take her clothes off. She didn't struggle or argue, she was laughing telling him what she was going to do to him sexually. The man snickered telling her he would see about that. He then had her nude body on the bed and reached for the camera.

"Sssh" Kathleen hushed him "Amanda might here us" she said putting her finger up to her lips.

"Is she a light sleeper?" the killer asked sounding concerned.

"No, she had a couple drinks tonight, probably couldn't hear us no matter what" Kathleen said giggling.

"You were in your room when he was here," Cal said opening his eyes.

"I was?" Amanda said surprised and shocked not remembering anyone else in the home that night.

"You had been drinking and were asleep," Cal continued.

"He was here alright," Cal said, blinking his eyes to see if he could pick up the face behind the man.

"I remember that night, I don't drink very often" Amanda told him.

"I don't remember meeting anyone though, he must have came after I was asleep" Amanda sat thinking.

"They were in this room together," Cal said closing his eyes again.

He saw the room again, this time picturing the huge back and frame of a man. He figured it had to be Barker, although, Barker's face was still unclear. The man had something in his hand. It looked like some sort of powder he stirred into Kathleen's drink. He sat on the edge of the bed, fiddling with his camera.

Kathleen came back into the room; he handed her the drink. She sipped the drink giggling handing it back to him. She had a gray housecoat on. The man stood up in front of her wrapping one arm around her tightly. The other hand pulled on her long blonde hair. He was already starting to get aggressive with her. He knew it was a matter of time before the drugs took affect and he could do what ever he wanted to her. He would just be patient and wait.

"So where were we" he teased getting rough with her.

Cal had a vision of the man slipping his hand into the gray housecoat worn by Kathleen. He slipped something into her pocket. The man grabbed her ripping her housecoat off exposing her nude body. She giggled taking it as teasing before he slid his pants down. He pushed her back onto the bed, getting on top of her. Her eyes rolled back in her head like she was having a seizure of some kind.

Cal opened his eyes taking a couple of minutes to adjust out of his trance. He then told Amanda about the man drugging Kathleen. He got up from the bed opening the folding closet door. He looked inside the neatly arranged closet. Kathleen had a lot of fancy clothing, jewelry and lingerie. Cal started pulling the hangers from one side to the other searching for the housecoat.

"What are you looking for?" Amanda asked standing behind him.

"A gray housecoat" Cal told her.

"Why?" she asked confused.

Cal pulled the housecoat off the hanger taking it to the bed.

"He put something in the pocket" Cal said reaching inside the pocket.

In the pocket was an empty bag with two empty capsules. They had been apart the contents were poured into Kathleen Logan's drink. He laid the housecoat, bag and the picture of Kathleen on the bed. He flipped the picture over, scrawled in black ink on the back of the picture was #10? He stared at the picture, the same handwriting that was on the bag of money. The same kind of writing was on that bill.

Who was this Barker and what kind of sick mind game was he playing. Was he taunting Cal to catch him? Playing with his mind, haunting his dreams. Was it possible that Barker's thoughts were being transmitted into Cal? If so did Barker also have Cal's thoughts? Amanda took the picture from his hand.

"How can you see the things you see?" she asked, flabbergasted at the picture and the thoughts that Cal had told her.

They moved back to the living room sipping coffee. Cal briefly told Amanda about his childhood. They talked about Colin Ray Barker and how they could find out who he was.

"What about the package in the car?" Amanda suggested.

"I don't know if you should get involved with this anymore" Cal told her, realizing the more he did the more it affected him.

She argued that she already knew everything and Kathleen was her friend. She told him that she deserved an ending to Kathleen Logan's life.

They talked about Cal's relationship with Eva Tucker. Why did Barker choose Eva, Amanda asked.

"Because Barker knew she was involved with me" He told

her, realizing he was taunting him now, because he knew Cal could see him and would be the only one that could stop him.

She finally convinced Cal that he should get the package out of the car. Cal left the apartment to get the package. He was still trying to think of what might be in the package. He had just gotten the package when Lieutenant Jim Mundale pulled up in his car.

"Shit" Cal muttered under his breath as he saw the detective get out of his car and approach him. He had to think of something fast. He had to confront and convince Mundale that he knew nothing. He put the package back down as Mundale approached. He made like he was getting his cigarettes out of the dash of the car.

What the hell would he tell Mundale? He took a glance at the apartment building. He saw Amanda standing on the deck of the apartment. She put her finger to her lips as if to tell him to be quiet. He knew he had to convince Mundale that he and Amanda were merely friends. Maybe, Mundale would just write if off as coincidence or maybe he would be very curious to why Cal showed up here.

"Hello Mr. Rushton" the detective replied being followed by another detective.

"Mr. Mundale" Cal said trying to sound calm with the surprise visitor.

"What brings you to this neck of the woods?" Mundale asked waiting for his reply.

"Just waiting for a friend," Cal said shutting the car door.

Cal lit up a cigarette, taking a long drag off of it. He felt awkward standing in the street. He couldn't imagine what kind of story he could come up with to convince Mundale being here as just Amanda's friend.

"Cal" he heard Amanda's voice coming out of the apartment building.

Mundale and the other detective turned to see her coming across the street. Mundale looked at her and back at Cal as if he had just found out something interesting.

Cal looked up a bit shocked that she would come out. He hoped she had come out to help him from unwanted questions. He knew Mundale had nothing on him, but he didn't need the detective suspicious.

"Hi detective Mundale" she said sweetly not giving him a chance to say anything.

"Hello Miss Riley" Mundale answered watching her come closer.

"You forgot your wallet," she said running up to Cal and giving him a kiss on the lips.

"Thanks" Cal said stunned, wondering what she was thinking.

Cal took the wallet and slid it into his back pocket. He didn't know what to say he was caught flat-footed and stood very awkward.

"Detective Mundale what brings you out here?" she said to him.

"Just passing by" the detective lied, looking for any sign of nervousness.

Cal noticed the other detective's eyes shift to the apartment building. He knew Mundale had come out for a reason, but after seeing them together he was sure Mundale's mind was thinking overtime.

"I do have a question for you Mr. Rushton" Mundale said turning his attention to Cal.

"Sure anything I can help you with," Cal said calmly, Amanda slipping her arm around his back.

Mundale noticed the affection that Amanda was giving to Cal. His suspicions grew as he watched the couple. He was very curious to know how they met, and how long they had known each other. Kathleen Logan had been dead for two weeks, as the Pathologist had stated in his report.

"How long have you two known each other?" Mundale said looking into Cal's eyes.

"That's the question?" Cal said mildly amused, but still very nervous to answer.

"About a week or so now" Amanda said trying to discourage the officer.

"But we've only been seeing each other now for a few days " Cal added.

"Sorry, that wasn't the question, that was more curiosity than anything"

Mundale said his face showing no expression.

Mundale knew that there was something a miss and he couldn't put his finger on it. The looks of Cal and Amanda just didn't fit.

"Have you been in to see Miss Tucker since the day before yesterday?" he

Asked, questioning Cal again.

"Just that once" Cal said, "When I came down to the station after to see you"

"What's this about?" Amanda asked her curiosity peaked.

"Miss Tucker has slipped into a coma," Mundale said waiting for Cal's reaction. He was baiting Amanda to see if she would take the bait.

"Her condition has worsened, she may not make it" Mundale told him.

"Have you thought of anything since we talked last?" Mundale asked prying for more information.

"Sorry detective, I haven't given it much thought" Cal told him.

Mundale and the other detective made their departure. Cal and Amanda stood by the car watching them disappear around the corner. Mundale sat in the car looking at the couple and still was very suspicious on how they met.

"Quick on your feet aren't you" Cal complimented her getting the package back out of the car.

"You know he's really suspicious now," Cal said referring to Mundale.

"Oh, I'm sure he is?" Amanda said looking back up the road.

"Let's see what's in this package," Cal said taking it and shaking it.

They walked back into the apartment together, glancing around to make sure Mundale didn't' return.

The package seemed light and didn't seem like it had much in it. Cal was very curious as to what was in here, another clue, money what?

"Thanks again" Cal said referring to her quick thinking.

"No problem, as I said I have to get to the bottom of this too" Amanda replied.

CHAPTER IV
DEADLY CLUES

Cal sat the box on the kitchen table. He was feeling very uneasy about opening the package. He wasn't sure what was inside, but whatever it was he was positive it would reveal some sort of clue.

"Well" Amanda said anxious to open the package.

Cal ripped open the brown paper revealing the box inside. An unforgettable smells rose from the box as Cal opened the lid. The smell was the smell of something rotting inside, but what?

"Jesus" Cal muttered as the smell lofted to his nostrils.

"What the hell is in there?" Amanda said scared to look inside.

On the top of the package was a piece of paper with a note.

"If you want what's here dig to the bottom," it said.

Cal didn't want to touch the blood stained paper. He carefully lifted the paper revealing a pair of blood soaked panties. Cal couldn't believe what he was seeing. Amanda felt faint at the sight of the Panties.

"Fuck" Cal cursed looking at Amanda.

Amanda pinched her nostrils to the smell, her stomach gurgling its disapproval. Cal picked up the panties between his forefinger and thumb gingerly lifting it onto the table. When he lifted the panties it unfolded the stench that was arising from the box. The decaying ear made Cal gag. Amanda started gagging, into the kitchen sink. Cal gagged looking into the bottom of the box.

A letter was neatly folded lying on the bottom of the package. The note had Cal's name scrawled on the top of it. He reached into the box gagging again. Amanda reached into the kitchen drawer pulling out a bag to put the ear into. The envelope felt heavy there was something rattled inside. Cal ripped open the envelope revealing a set of keys. Not at all what he had bargained for as clues. Cal looked at Amanda confused at what they were seeing and opening.

"What's this?" Cal said the keys falling to the kitchen table.

They were both in shock and horrified but the sight of the bloody ear.

There was a note inside the envelope a strange cryptic note.
Remember this ear...I think it should be clear...
Where you once nibbled...There is no more...
The panties I fear...Are from the same as the ear...
Did I make myself clear...? Don't mean to steer you wrong...
A gift waits in the place you will find... Can you find me...?
Or do I torture your thoughts...I will haunt you forever...
Until the very end...guess who...

The note was unsigned Cal read it aloud. His thoughts and premonitions about Colin Ray Barker were vivid in his mind.

What kind of a lunatic was this man to go to this extent? He was looking for Cal to catch him, wanting to be caught. Cal felt really ill looking at the stuff on the table. His head was pounding again, this time he could feel the room spinning.

"This is really sick" Amanda stood mortified by what had taken place.

Cal took the bag from Amanda placing the panties and decaying ear inside. Then he picked up the box and not putting them in the bag as well. He could still feel the room spinning but managed to control his emotions. He was more upset that these clues were aimed at him with his name on them.

"What do we do now?" Amanda said very puzzled.

Cal got waves of pain suddenly, thoughts again that weren't his. This time it was Eva being raped, beaten and tortured. The same man was prodding her with a screwdriver. She screamed but nothing came out. The man taped her mouth shut. He pulled out a razor sharp hunting knife, glinting in the light. She screamed in pain but nothing came out only tears in her bloodshot eyes. The man was not going to stop until she was dead.

"Let's see what else you got bitch" the man hissed.

He grabbed her ear lopping it off with one deadly stroke. Cal felt faint as he came back around. Amanda was standing over him as he collapsed onto the floor. Amanda ran to the sink getting a damp face cloth. He could feel himself passing out but couldn't stop the blackness coming over him.

"Cal, Cal" she repeated trying to get a response.

He answered telling her the ear belonged to Eva, as well as the panties. He told her that he believed Barker didn't kill Eva, because it was a message to him. The key's he wasn't sure about, but he assumed they were some kind of sick gift given to Cal to keep him interested. He noticed that the keys were to a car; God knows what they would find in that he thought. He hadn't told Amanda about the money. But, he did now. Amanda sat stunned as the tale twisted and turned in odd directions, never giving enough clues to solve.

Cal wasn't sure where the car was; wiping the blood off the key chain it revealed keys to a Mercedes. He was obviously stunned by all the things that were happening. He said nothing, as he sat looking at the key chain. He wanted this all to stop but it was obviously to late and getting more personal by the minute. He warned Amanda that she should think about going out of town and visiting friends or relatives for a while until he got it sorted out.

"Maybe we should call the police," Amanda suggested.

"Don't you think I've already thought of that?" Cal said looking up at her.

"If we do, the police either won't believe us or they will try to put the blame on me" Cal told her.

"The evidence all points at me so far, whoever this man is he wants me" Cal stopped sitting down on a chair. "We have to find Barker first, before he kills again," he told her.

Amanda was one step ahead of him pulling out the phone book. She began leafing through the pages of the book looking for the last name Barker. Maybe, a relative or something would come out in the book and they may find the whereabouts of Colin Ray Barker that way.

"Why didn't I think of that?" he said watching her leaf through the phone book.

"A. Barker, Betty Barker, Steven Barker, Barker's Garage. That's all the listings for Barker" she told him.

Barker's Garage, is there an address?" Cal asked thinking about seeing Colin Ray in his coveralls. She looked closer at the address.

"1412 Greenbow Lane" she said.

They put another bag over the already bagged ear and panties. Amanda opened the freezer door on the fridge. He placed the bag inside closing the door. Amanda proceeded to scour and disinfect the kitchen table all the time gagging. Cal debated on going to Barker's Garage by himself. He also thought about calling Lieutenant Mundale to meet him there. He dismissed the thought; This Barker may not even be the right one. The ear and panties were evidence and to hold them back from Mundale could be considered withholding information relevant to the case. One thing for certain, Cal had seen Barker's nametag on a pair of coveralls worn by a man at a service station. That's where Colin Ray met Kathleen Logan. Now he had to find out if it was the same Barker or if it was just another wild goose chase. Things were getting more serious then ever now with the recent box containing the ears.

Cal still thought about Mundale, but it all may point back to Cal. The point being, Cal had a near death experience and was with Eva Tucker and was acting very strangely and committed to the mental ward of the hospital. Cal could be considered a suspect and at this time he was. But, he had no idea of what was going on if he brought the information forward it could possibly implicate himself.

"Maybe, I should go by myself," Cal suggested referring to the garage.

"Oh, no you don't I'm not staying here with that thing in the icebox" Amanda said scouring out the sink. "Besides you may need my help if there's some sort of confrontation" Amanda added.

"Maybe, I should just call the number?" Cal said, inquiring if he can speak to Colin Ray Barker.

"And say what, ask if this is the murdering bastard Barker?"

Amanda said in an angry tone. "Besides he already knows about you," she said making sense to Cal.

"This son of a bitch is sick," Cal said in reply.

The two of them left the apartment again, both in a quiet solitude of their own thoughts. Cal opened the car door for Amanda shutting it behind her.

"Are you okay?" Cal asked sitting in the driver's seat.

"Considering" she nodded all that's happened.

He got out the black wallet she had given him earlier.

"Oh, here's your wallet" Cal fished it out giving it to her.

"That's not mine, it's one I found in the apartment earlier probably one of Kathleen's dates," she said taking the wallet.

"When did you find it?" Cal asked curiosity getting him.

"Can't remember for sure" she paused "I hid it in the cookie jar, waiting for someone to call for it back".

"Open it!" Cal said expecting the unexpected.

"Oh shit!" Amanda said opening the wallet "I forgot all about it until

Mundale showed up," she said opening the wallet.

"What's in it?" Cal asked his curiosity peaked.

"No, identification" she paused "Wait".

"What is it?" Cal leaned over trying to view what she was looking at.

"Money and a wad of it" Amanda said looking at the bundle of bills.

"Let me guess one hundred dollar bills" Cal surmised, knowing that's what she was going to find.

"How did you know?" Amanda said, remembering what he had told her "oh right" she hesitated.

"All the money I found was one hundred dollar bills," Cal told her.

"Is there a not or something written on the bills," he asked.

"No note, but yes there is something on the bills," she said taking the money out of the wallet.

"There's a word on each bill" Amanda noted.

"Nine bills, one for each victim, hurry find me before it's ten" the bills read from top to bottom.

"Just as I suspected Kathleen is not the first?" Cal said, knowing now they had a serial killer.

"Nine bills, nine victims" Amanda said counting out the bills.

"This wallet must have been left at your place by Barker the night Kathleen disappeared" Cal said looking at her, thinking out loud.

"The police came and scoured her room looking for some kind of clue" she said "but I hid the wallet thinking whoever it belonged to would be back and I forgot it was there, that was before Kathleen disappeared".

"Why didn't you look inside until now?" He asked.

"Too much excitement, just forgot all about it," She added, looking through the bills again.

"That picture had #10 on it" he said deep in thought.

"So you think Barker planned this all along?" she said opening the glove box and tossing the wallet inside.

"Whoever Barker is he must be wealthy and ruthless," she suggested.

"Do you know where Greenbow Lane is?" Cal asked.

"It's off the main street down towards the waterfront," she told him, thinking about the address.

"There's only one garage that I know of in that area," Cal said thinking about the little garage. "It's a run down shit hole of a place," he remembered getting gas there once.

The two drove downtown turning down Greenbow Lane. It was a short road between two other main streets, running north to south. The road was in the busy part of the business sector. The small garage was run down, rusty gas pumps looked like they had been out of service for a long time. A small sign hung in the garage door. Barker's Garage, below it repairs and oil changes. It didn't looked like it had much business, or whoever owned just used it as a front for something else.

"This can't be the right Barker" Cal said looking at the front of the run down place.

He parked the car across the street from the rundown garage. They sat watching the place looking for some sign of movement from inside. A four-wheel drive pickup pulled into the yard. A man stepped out of the truck; it wasn't Barker that Cal was sure of. Maybe he was a relative of Colin Ray it wouldn't hurt to investigate. The man flipped the sign on the front door to open and went inside. The man was wearing greasy overalls and an old stained baseball hat. They watched him a bit longer; lights came on in the Bay of the garage. They could see a car on a hoist in the Bay of the garage.

Cal rolled down the window and listened to the sound of the compressor start up from inside.

"I'm going in to see him," Cal said opening the door. "You stay here in case there's trouble," he told her.

"Okay" she said crawling over into the driver's seat.

Cal crossed the street, he felt nervous, and he wasn't sure how to approach the man inside. But he knew that the man inside wasn't Colin Ray Barker.

He reached the door of the garage, looking back at Amanda. Amanda watched him disappear inside the garage. Inside there was an old cash register, a glass counter top with newspapers strewn over the top of it. A pop machine that didn't looked like it saw any money in a long time.

The place didn't look like it was cleaned in a long time.

"Hello" Cal announced his arrival.

The man was working under the car. He popped his head from around the tire of the car to see who had come in. He had an old greasy ball cap on. His beard and mustache didn't seem to have been trimmed in a long time. The man was big with massive hands and sunken black eyes. His nose was bent as if broken on more than one occasion.

"What can I do for you?" He asked Cal.

"I'm looking for Colin Ray Barker" Cal told him bluntly.

He came from under the car wiping his hands off on an oily rag. The man was in his late early forties, Cal guessed as he came out. The man's face was covered with a matted beard. He was covered with grease, fingers and hands and even on his face.

"I'm looking for Colin Ray" Cal said again, unsure if the man had heard him.

"Hell boy, Colin is in the big house, last I heard" the man said through his yellow stained teeth.

"Is he a brother of yours?" Cal asked, trying to get as much information as he could.

"No, he's just a cousin of mine" the man answered "My names Clive Barker, lot of people come in looking for Colin getting us mixed up".

"What was Colin Ray send to prison for?" Cal inquired trying to be as friendly as he could.

"Why you looking for him?" he paused "he done something wrong again?" The big man said continuing to wipe his hands on the oily rag.

"No a friend of mine disappeared, he was the last one to see her" Cal told him, "just thought he might know his whereabouts".

"Pearl might know where he's at," the man said spitting on the floor.

"Whose Pearl?" Cal asked looking around at the cluttered garage.

"My wife, Colin Ray's sister" he said not embarrassed by marrying his own cousin.

"Where's Pearl at?" Cal asked him.

"Just hang on we'll give her a jingle, see if she's home" the big hands of Clive Barker reached for the phone.

Cal waited patiently for Clive to call his wife. He listened briefly to the conversation, picking up bits and pieces. What he heard gave him doubt that this was the same Colin Ray Barker. Maybe, but the chances of two men with the same name would be highly coincidental.

Colin Ray was uncommon and hard to phantom another Colin Ray Barker. This man's background didn't sound like he had the neither wealth nor intelligence to do something like this. Colin noticed the nametag on Barker's overalls. It was the same as Colin Ray Barker's tag the same style. Clive Barker hung up the phone and turned to Cal.

"Colin Ray is dead," he said point blank, "died in jail".

"How come you didn't know that?" Cal asked him point blank.

"Me and the Mrs. don't live together anymore" Clive grinned his yellow stained teeth.

"I'm sorry," Cal said "When did he die, did she say," Cal asked finding it strange that the man he thought was the killer was actually dead.

"Few weeks back, New Years Day to be exact" Clive said, walking back in to work on the car on the ramp.

Cal listened intently gathering more information. Apparently, Colin Ray Barker died on New Years Day, by hanging himself in prison. By the time the guards found him he was already dead. It suddenly dawned on Cal that it was the same day he tried to end his own life by hanging. Was this all just a coincidence, or something more bizarre?

"Can I ask you one more question Mr. Barker" Cal asked trying to get as much information before he left.

"Sure thing" the man seemed generally a friendly sort although he might seem a bit rough around the edges.

"Did Colin Ray ever work for you?" he asked Barker.

"Yeah, for a short while, had to fire him" Clive told him "He was stealing things out of customers cars. Don't like thieves much" Barker commented.

Cal thanked Barker for his time and left the garage, he was now even more confused. He crossed the street as a big limousine pulled into the driveway of Barker's Garage. Must have a good clientele Cal thought as the bay door slide open. He shook his head in disgust; Amanda could see the disappointment on his face. She was disappointed as well as relieved. The whole ordeal had made her scared and worried. She had never had this kind of excitement in her life before. She crawled back over the passenger's seat as Cal opened the driver's door.

"No luck?" she asked knowing what he would say.

Cal told her about the conversation. He told her Colin Ray was a small time thief and not the right man. He explained to her about the patch on the coveralls, saying maybe someone had stolen the coveralls from Colin Ray Barker.

"He hung himself in prison" Cal said bracing his hands against the steering wheel of the car.

"It must be a different Colin Ray Barker," the exasperated Amanda said.

"That was my thought too". "But what are the chances of someone having the same name Colin Ray" Cal said trying to think things out clearly.

"When did he die?" Amanda asked curiously.

"New Years Day" Cal suddenly got pins and needles in his had, a chill ran down his spine.

"What's going on here?" Cal said thinking about his and Colin Rays same fate on New Years Day.

He got a strange feeling; Amanda sat silently watching him. Was this all to do with his near death and Colin Ray's death? Were they somehow connected, was there another man that also attempted suicide the same day. Strange thoughts rolled through his mind. Bizarre was more like it. He voiced his thoughts to Amanda waiting for her insight.

Cal felt suddenly speechless thinking about the day of death, did Colin Ray Barker pass him by in that dark space. Was it him that he felt when he was falling? Colin Ray Barker's death was, Colin Ray Barker passing along messages to him.

"I'm speechless, I really don't know what to say or think" she paused.

"Maybe, it's all coincidence" she said really unsure, setting there thinking about it.

I should find out more about Colin Ray. I still have no idea if the man that's dead and the man that haunts me are the same man.

Cal got back out of his car heading back towards the garage. Clive was busy talking to the man that drove the limo when Cal came back in. He didn't want to interrupt the conversation so he waited until they were done talking. The two men were haggling over the costs to repair the limo. Clive Barker if he was anything he was an expert at haggling over prices and costs for parts. Maybe, that's how he kept the shop going by gouging people like this one.

"I can't afford that," the man told Barker.

"You can't afford not to, if you don't your gonna have more problems later on" Barker argued.

The two came to a compromise, the limo driver getting back into his car.

"Hang on a minute" Barker said following the driver into the bay and opening the door.

Barker let the car out and came back into the office. Barker's demeanor didn't seem as friendly this time around, maybe it was haggling over the cost with the customer, but he definitely changed.

"Did you forget something?" Barker asked him.

"I need some more information on Colin Ray," he told Barker, trying not to be too forceful.

"What the hell you need, he's dead," Barker said unsure of what Cal was looking for.

"Would it be alright to talk with Pearl?" he asked the man.

"I just need to find out more on Colin Ray" Cal told him wanting to know More about what had happened and why he was in prison. The big man looked like he was about to lose his temper. Instead he reached down and picked up the phone.

"Pearl" he said "This here fella is asking a bunch of questions about Colin Ray, he wants to talk to you" he paused handing the phone to Cal.

Pearl seemed very friendly on the phone and was willing to meet Cal. She gave Cal her address and asked him to come for tea. Cal hung up the phone and thanked Clive Barker for his help.

Clive Barker rough exterior was just a front for an honest hard workingman. He had a simple philosophy, was to work hard, please his clients and respect them. Although, his shop looked run down, Clive Barker didn't believe in all the modern technology. He saved his money and was fairly well off. He gave his ex wife Pearl everything she wanted. In return Pearl was his bookkeeper and cleaned his apartment once a week.

Clive put one of his big paws out to shake Cal's hand. Cal accepted and left the premises walking back to the car.

Amanda was sitting deep in thought about Cal. She was concerned about his weird affliction. She thought about all the events that had happened since meeting him this morning. She was already mentally, and emotionally exhausted, she couldn't imagine how Cal felt. Cal sat in the driver's seat handing Amanda a piece of paper with Pearl Barkers address on it. Maybe, this would shed some light on Colin Ray Barker. Hopefully, meeting Pearl Barker would lead them to the real killer or at least give some sort of explanation as to why Cal was having these visions and dreams.

"She would like us to come for tea" Cal said referring to Pearl Barker.

Amanda looked at the address and the directions given to Cal. She knew where the address was and folded the paper up sitting it on her lap.

"Can we stop by the café for a minute" she asked realizing she had promised to come back to work.

She had to make arrangements to make sure someone would look after the Café while she was gone.

"Oh that's right you have to go back to work," Cal asked remembering her promise to be back in a couple hours.

"No, I have good people working for me" Amanda said. "I just need to take some time off," Amanda said pausing. "I want to get to the bottom of this thing as much as you do," she said looking at the garage as they pulled away.

"And all this time I thought it was my bubbly personality" he joked.

She laughed as the drove across town to her shop. Amanda stopped into the café; Cal came in and sipped a coffee while Amanda made arrangements. Amanda got the cook to make some breakfast for them. They sat quietly looking out the window of the café. Eggs, toast, and hash browns with ham were served. Cal didn't realize how hungry he was as he sat down to eating.

"Do you think Colin Ray's death is being used as an excuse to throw off the police"? Amanda said putting down her fork.

"I'm not sure about anything, but it is a possibility" Cal said taking another mouthful of hash browns.

"You have a great place here" he complimented her.

"It's got its good points and bad points," Amanda admitted. "I have to admit I don't have any personal life," she said.

The two ate the rest of their meals, chatting idly about anything but Colin Ray. They talked about their families, friends and acquaintances.

An hour passed by they decided they had better get over to Pearl Barker's. One of the waitresses whispered something to Amanda before they left. Cal saw them looking over his way. Amanda looked embarrassed as the waitress giggled.

"What was that all about?" Cal asked her as they made their way to the car.

"She thought we made a handsome couple" Amanda turned red and felt embarrassed.

"If she only knew," Amanda said referring to the whole ordeal and reason they were together.

Cal said nothing in response, but thought if things were different he would be very interested in Amanda. He thought all women he dated liked to drink and do drugs.

Amanda was different, sincere, sweet and wholesome. Amanda Riley was very beautiful, although reserved and shy. She would make a great wife and mother some day Cal thought. They didn't speak much on the drive to Pearl Barker's. Mostly just reading directions to get to the street she lived on.

Chapter V

Colin Ray Barker

They pulled in front of a neat small bungalow. Cal got out of the car, watching Amanda put lipstick on in the mirror. He opened the passenger's door for her. The yard was well cared for neat bushes lined the driveway. The bungalow was tucked away on a quiet sub-division at the very end of the street.

"Ready" he said realizing he couldn't remember the last time he opened a car door for anyone.

"Thanks" she said smiling.

"Do I look alright?" she asked fluffing her hair.

"Gorgeous" he said catching himself and realizing he was honestly enjoying her company in this bizarre journey.

Cal rang the doorbell of the small bungalow. Pearl Barker answered the door. Her appearance was not at all what Cal had imagined. He imagined a plump elderly lady with graying hair. Instead, Pearl Barker was slim, shapely for her age and her red hair was neat and well kept. She smiled opening the door and inviting them in.

"You must be Cal," She said extending her hand.

"Mrs. Barker" he said taking her hand.

"Oh please call me Pearl," she said noticing Amanda.

"Who is this lovely creature?" She said extending her hand to Amanda.

"Hi, I'm Amanda" she said promptly.

"Come right in, Tea's on," she said.

Pearl escorted them into a brightly lit, cheerful living room. The house was well furnished, decorated with nothing but the best. Pearl excused herself and returned with tray, teapot and cups. She disappeared back into the kitchen and returned with cookies and cake. She sat down motioning them to help themselves. Cal looked around the house at all the antiques and collectibles she had amassed. It was evident she took pride in her surroundings and liked to feel comfortable. Family pictures on the wall, mostly two to three generations before her time hung to accent the antiques.

"So how did you know Colin Ray?" she said taking a chair that faced the two of them.

"I had a few dreams and woke up with his name in my head" Cal said not lying.

"Are you clairvoyant?" she asked him.

"I'm not sure what I am anymore," he told her picking up the teapot and pouring himself a cup.

"It's a funny thing you asking about Colin Ray and having dreams with him in them Mr. Rushton" she said looking as if you was in the distant somewhere. "You see Colin Ray had an accident a couple years ago before his death" she continued. "After the accident he had strange dreams and nightmares" she added. "He had nightmares about the wildest things, he told no one but me about his dreams". She stopped momentarily then continued. "Dreams of death and the like" she told them. "They were dreams that scared the Hell out of him, dreams he mostly kept to himself". "He told me about some of them, I was concerned for his mental health at that point". He had no place to stay, so he stayed here with me for a few months. I thought maybe staying with me might help him and the dreams might stop. But, the dreams only got worse; I can remember being awakened in the night from his cries. Poor Colin Ray was a troubled soul, and there was nothing I could do to help ease the dreams. He would often say he wished he were dead; at least the dreams would end.

Cal and Amanda sat listening to her. The story sounded a lot like Cal's. Cal couldn't get over the fact that this man had similar experiences.

"Poor Colin Ray, had the most awful headaches. He rarely slept after a few months for fear of the dreams. Colin Ray wasn't a bad man, he made some foolish mistakes". She told them. "He got involved with the wrong bunch and then the headaches didn't let up and he didn't know what he was doing before they caught him and sent him off to prison.

She went on to tell them that Colin Ray had brushes with the law for petty theft, burglary and forgery. He had become addicted to drugs and had to make money to support his increasing habit. After the accident he was accused of rape and murder. He came to me and told me he was being framed for something he didn't do. He never went into a lot of the details with me. But, he was charged with the rape and murder of a well known

Businesswoman. Colin Ray told me before he went to prison that he didn't know the young woman. He said that he had cleaned up his act after the accident and was trying to make a new life. He wanted help, so a young lady helped him get off the streets and drugs.

Pearl bent down and picked up a photo album.

"This was Colin Ray's picture," she said pointing to a picture of him.

The picture was fairly recent; he was going through a lot of stuff at that time. Look at the face, I never seen the pour soul smile for months at a time.

"It was taken three month's before he sent to prison" she told them.

"How long was he in prison?" Amanda asked looking at his picture.

"Six month's before he died" Pearl said a noticeable note of sadness in her voice.

She went on with her story about Colin Ray. She told them Colin Ray got a ten-year sentence for conspiracy and theft. He received another 25 years to life for the conviction of murder. She told them she saw him a week before he died. She had flown down to the state prison to see him. "His eyes, I'll never forget" she started to weep.

Amanda got up to comfort the woman. Taking her hands in hers.

"They were black and lifeless, he spoke very little" she started weeping more. "The last thing he said to me as I was leaving was, Please help me," she said breaking down again.

"I felt so helpless, there was nothing I could do" she went on "But, I can honestly say I saw death in his eyes that day" she told them.

Cal took another look at the picture. Colin Ray was not at all what he had envisioned. Yet he seemed vaguely familiar to him. Colin Ray's hair was black, with a neatly trimmed beard. His blue eyes gave Cal a chill. By the picture he could only guess that Colin Ray was probably six feet, six one. His build was slender yet masculine. He was wearing a white shirt with a tattoo on his right wrist. Cal strained to tell what was written there. He could tell they were words but what did they say. Cal was curious about the tattoo, he thought he had seen it somewhere before, but still couldn't put him finger on it.

"What is this tattoo on his arm?" he inquired, staring at the picture trying to make it out.

"Oh, that's something strange" she said pausing. "Above it say's meet the devil. In the center of the circle were his initials CRB, and below it the word Brotherhood. " She told them.

Cal looked at the symbol it was weird, but he thought he had seen it somewhere before, maybe in his dreams he thought.

"He had that one put on his arm shortly after his accident" she told them, referring to Colin Rays near death incident "He thought that he had beaten the devil" she stopped.

"But, the Devil beat him in the end" she finished.

"I wish I could tell you more, but Colin Ray got more and more withdrawn near the end".

"He did say that he never hurt that woman, he said he loved her" she picked up a Kleenex blowing her nose. "One strange thing though, Colin Ray never had much money or anything" she told them. "But the last going off he had money to burn" she spoke more.

"Colin Ray bought me a new car, some of the furniture you see here. He told me not to concern myself with money any more that he had lots". She went on. "Rarely did he spend any money on himself. I tried to warn him that he would get caught in whatever it was he was doing" So Colin Ray started sending things to me, you name it money, jewelry". "That just pissed Clive off more and more, he knew Colin Ray was sending me things". "He started calling Colin Ray names, like Tattoo boy and other vulgar names".

Cal sat listening to the woman. Money, cars, notes, all

sounded so familiar to him. Cal closed his eyes putting his hand on Colin Ray's picture. What happened next terrified Cal? The vision was instant and violent. It left Cal paralyzed and shaking. Colin Ray Barker wasn't the man responsible at all for the murders. Colin Ray was working on a car in Barker's Garage. He was cleaning the interior of the car. The Cadillac's back seat floor was littered with garbage. He heard screaming as he continued to clean. He was having one of his visions. Colin Ray sat speechless in the backseat of the car holding onto his head. He saw death; to be exact the screams were from different victims. Victim's cries for mercy as Colin Ray wiped down the leather seats with cleaner. This time there was pleas from the victims. He sat in shock pulling out a pair of bloody panties from under the passenger's seat. He could see a struggle inside the car. All he could see was the outline of a struggle through steamed glass of the car. He heard the victim's pleas of mercy, the slap across the face, which echoed, in his head. Then the pleas stopped followed by sobbing. Then mercifully silence.

Colin Ray was witnessing a murder, so was the money given to him a gift to keep him shut up. What other explanation was there with his new found wealth. Colin Ray Barker had struggled through life as a petty theft, now all of a sudden he had money to burn. Did he get involved in something illegal? Cal really didn't think so Colin Ray was the brightest of people, but he wouldn't stoop to anything as low as murder.

Cal opened his eyes but couldn't stop shaking. Amanda sat by his side easing him back against the back of the sofa. He was soaked with sweat, his heart raced. Pearl arrived with a damp facecloth.

"Cal, Cal" Amanda said rubbing his face with the damp face cloth.

"What did you see?" Pearl asked looking very worried.

Cal was still shaking and couldn't shake the thoughts out of his head. He couldn't believe what he had just seen. Colin Ray was not guilty the only thing he was guilty of was witnessing the murder.

"All those voices" he whispered, his voice low and strained.

"Voices" Amanda repeated.

"Whose voices?" Pearl asked "Colin Ray's" she asked

"He was there, he felt the same thing I did" Cal explained, trying to explain Colin Ray didn't do anything wrong, except being at the wrong place at the wrong time.

He sat up putting his head between his knees. The three sat a few minutes while Cal gathered his thoughts. Cal briefly told them the events that had happened. She sat and listened waiting for him to finish. He was weak and the headache was coming on again. Cal couldn't explain what he just saw; once again he couldn't see the killer only visions of what was going on in the back of the Limo.

"Do you think Colin Ray is responsible for any of those deaths?" she asked

Finally, hoping that Cal would say no.

"No, he just saw the deaths the same as me" Cal continued. "I don't think that he had anything to do with the deaths at all," he added. "He was there, but only as a witness". "I'm still not sure why I keep seeing him in my dreams, but I finally think I have it figured out.

The day he died was the day I tried to kill myself. We passed each other in death and he passed along what he had seen to me. He wanted me to solve this murder and to redeem himself for not going to the police and reporting what he had seen.

Pearl Barker sat stunned for a moment, but she was glad they thought that Colin Ray was innocent. That meant a lot to her to think her brother was innocent of the crimes of murder. After all she didn't think he had it in him to kill, he was a kind enough human, just struggling in life to get by.

Cal and Amanda left Pearl Barker's home with nothing more than the fact that Colin Ray Barker wasn't the killer. He like Cal had merely seen them in his visions. There was a possibility that these thoughts and nightmares were those of Colin Ray Barker passed onto Cal Rushton. Was it possible that someone else posed as Colin Ray, he doubted that? Whoever was responsible for the deaths was still out there and haunting Cal. Taunting him to catch him. Amanda drove as Cal rested his exhausted mind. He closed his eyes as they drove to Cal's apartment. Cal was so exhausted now, his head throbbed, and his mind wouldn't shut down.

Inside Cal's apartment Amanda prepared some supper from the meager supplies Cal had for groceries. Cal lay on the sofa and drifted off to sleep. Amanda was beginning to worry about him, as his last vision seems to take its toll on Cal. He was so exhausted he left his shoes on as he put his weary head down on the pillow.

Amanda hoped he wouldn't have anymore-violent dreams or nightmares. She slipped his shoes off and found a blanket to cover him over with. Cal's face was pale; his eyes had dark circles under them. She tucked the blanket around him, giving him a peck on the cheek.

She thought if only things were different she could have fallen in love with this guy. After all Cal Rushton was a handsome, polite and sincere man.

Cal woke after a couple of hours of sound sleep. He was exhausted he couldn't recall falling asleep. He had no dreams that he could recall. He looked over and saw Amanda asleep in the armchair. He got up, waking her instantly.

"Feeling any better?" she asked.

"Yeah, but I'm starving" he told her; he could smell the food she had cooked.

He looked outside it was now dark. "What time is it?" he asked wandering towards the patio doors.

"It's almost 10pm, I made some soup for supper" she said turning to warm it up.

"It smells good," he said looking at the two settings on the table.

Amanda served him soup and made some sandwiches out of ham and lettuce from the fridge.

"Sorry there wasn't much to choose from" she told him.

They ate, Cal enjoying the supper, but mostly her company. In the back of his mind he wished none of the incidents had taken place. But, if they didn't he would never have met her. After supper they did the dishes together. They sat on the sofa together watching the news.

"What's next?" she asked looking at him, wondering if he had any plans.

"I can drive you home anytime you want" he told her clicking off the TV.

"No hurry, I can spend the night if that's okay" she told him.

"I'll give you my bed" Cal said realizing he was excited that she was staying over.

They sat and talked about what they were going to do next. They even discussed calling detective Mundale. But, the story was so strange that he wouldn't believe it. Amanda suggested getting some concrete evidence first before they went to the law. Cal mentioned the garage, Barker's and the Cadillac. He knew that Colin Ray had worked there briefly and thought maybe one of his client's cars held the key to the real killer. He wondered how many more victims would die before the killer or killers were caught. The killer was not going to stop now and Cal could sense it.

He knew that Colin Ray had taken the secrets to his grave with him. He didn't want to end up like Colin Ray. Colin Ray in the end was losing a grip on reality and nothing made sense to him anymore. Cal thought about that and the fact that he was having the same symptoms scared him.

"Nine victims and counting" Cal said, trying to think of where the killer would strike next.

"I wonder who all those other victims are?" Amanda said, trying to help him figure out if there was any kind of connection, or just random killings. "We know of Kathleen and Ray's girlfriend," she said.

The phone rang cutting the conversation short. Cal got up answered the phone his face turning pale. Amanda watched his facial expressions and knew that he had heard some bad news.

"I understand," he said, shaking his head.

"It was Detective Mundale," he said hanging up the phone.

"Eva is dead he wants me to meet him at the hospital" Cal explained. "That's ten" Cal said shaking his head.

"It's not your fault" she tried to reassure him.

"I know but, the killer is giving me clues to me" Cal said. "Its my job now to figure out those clues and try to stop him" he said matter of fact.

"I wonder why Mundale said he needed me there" Cal looked puzzled and concerned.

"Do you want to drop me off first" Amanda asked not really wanting to go home.

"No" Cal said "You're staying close by the hospital, we can get this thing figured out together" He told her. "I'm not sure what's going on but I don't trust leaving you by yourself," he said indicating that the killer may come after her.

They drove off to meet Mundale at the hospital. The drive over then went over what they guessed Mundale might want from Cal. They could come up with nothing concrete that they thought he might want. Mundale was a stern, play it by the book Policeman. He may just have some follow up questions regarding Eva.

Jim Mundale was in the hospital room of Eva Tucker. The scene was a crime scene. Eva Tucker was smothered while she was lying in a coma. A note was left on the bedside tray, yet another cryptic note. Mundale had been working on this case for quite sometime. He was aware that the killer or killers were still at large. He knew that quite possibly there was a serial killer on the loose. He thought about Cal Rushton and there was something strange about him and his ability to know a lot more than he admitted to.

Detective Mundale had to dig down a little deeper and find out of Rushton knew more than he was letting on. He was aware of five murders related with the same trademarks. But the cryptic note spooked him. It was the first such note left behind by the killer.

Do I have your ear?
Hickory dickory dock
The clock struck ten
She was the next
On my endless list
There is one thing for sure
To catch me is the cure
Hickory dickory dock
In my doctors smock
I can fool everyone

Except for the guy named Cal
He is the key
To finding me
Hickory dickory dock

The note was not a complete mystery to him. The ear meant the loping off of Eva and Kathleen's ears. As well as the other three victims that he knew of. Endless list meant the killer would continue until he was caught or dead. He faked being a doctor to gain access into the room. Cal must be Cal Rushton; he is the key…. Detective Mundale had been working homicide for the past five years. He thought he had seen everything, until this killer came along. It was safe to say he was dealing with a serial killer. But, he couldn't inform the press they would eat it up. But, how would he catch him. Up until now the only leads he had were either dead or dead end.

Detective Mundale watched the forensic team working on the room. The ward of the hospital was shut down to keep the media out. They would of course search for clues, fingerprints or any thing out of the ordinary. They had to check everything they could, Maybe a smudged print on the letter. He slipped the note into a plastic bag to be sent for testing. He had a hunch that something was up with Rushton when he saw him with Amanda Riley. The other coincidence was Eva Tucker's lifeless body. Eva and Cal Rushton were a couple a short time ago. Now she was dead and Cal was with one of the other victim's roommates, Amanda. Mundale at one point was convinced he had the killer behind bars. The killer he thought was Colin Ray Barker. All the evidence pointed in his direction after the death of another victim. But, the death toll started to begin again in the New Year.

Detective Mundale had questioned all the nurses that were on duty. Other patients on the floor were questioned, as were doctors. No one had seen anyone strange enter Eva Tucker's room. He had to find some evidence fast and arrest the killer. If the media got a hold of this the whole city would be in panic. He had taken the position in Fox Creek to get away from big city crime. But here he was in the middle of what appeared to be a serial killer. He had brought his wife and two children, from Boston to settle here. They were sure that the lifestyle would be good for all of them. It wasn't up until the past year that things had gone bad. With now six deaths, with only one prominent, Kathleen Logan, the killer had no fixed lifestyle for his victims. The others were normal girls, with normal jobs except Colin Ray's girlfriend. The only connection seemed to be Cal Rushton.

He ruled out Rushton as the actual killer, but could he be an accomplice, he doubted that as well. The camera flashed again, Mundale needed some air. He had taken the guard off Eva Tuckers room only last night. Now she was dead and he felt partly responsible for her death. Somebody must have been watching the room. Someone had to have known Eva Tucker was no longer being watched, but whom?

Cal and Amanda left the apartment heading for the hospital. This whole thing to Cal was making him edgy, nervous and sick. Pearl Barker had warned him that Colin Ray had gone insane the last few weeks before he was arrested. She told Cal that Colin Ray had almost seemed relieved to be sent to prison. Would he too crack under the barrage of nightmares, deaths and terror?

Amanda sat silent on the way to the hospital. She asked him if he was okay. He gave her a one-word answer, still deep in thought. She could see him deep in thought and was worried about his mental stability. Snowflakes danced off the windshield of the car. The weather was crazy, it just kept snowing on and off for the past couple of weeks. Amanda wanted to get out of this mess, but she also wanted to help Cal find the killer.

They drove into Seaside Memorial Hospital, parking the car. This was the same hospital Cal Rushton had ended up after his suicide attempt. This killer had to be found soon before Cal went crazy. It was like a nightmare that never ended. The only rest he had gotten was four hours that he just had. Cal was speechless; Eva Tuckers death was an obvious message to him. But why was the killer giving him messages? Was it because they knew each other's thoughts? One thing was clear the killer knew more about Cal than he knew about him. Cal wasn't sure how much Mundale knew, if he knew anything at all.

"Mundale will have a ton of questions," he told Amanda as they walked down the front lobby.

"Let me do all the talking, I mean this concerns me not you" he warned her.

"I've been thinking the same thing, I'm just here to support you and your decisions," she told him, concerned about Mundale may ask.

They walked down the corridor; Jim Mundale was standing outside the hospital room of Eva Tucker. He held a notepad and was scribbling something down as they came up the hall. Amanda reached down and took a hold of Cal's hand. Cal felt her gentle touch, accepting her hand in his. He felt odd that he had these feelings for her. He knew he was starting to care a lot for her and she liked him as well. It wasn't fair that all the things that happened were the things that brought them together.

"Mr. Rushton, Miss Riley" Mundale said sliding his notepad into his breast pocket.

"I'm sorry to call you in here to ask questions, but I'm hoping you may be able to give us some information" Mundale said stopping them in the doorway.

"I hope I can help detective," Cal said stopping in front of him.

"First off Eva has been murdered" Mundale told him he watched looking for some kind of expression from Cal.

Cal's jaw dropped open, he couldn't believe that the killer had come to the hospital to murder her. The murderer now had ten and this one was personal.

"There was a note left behind, I'm hoping you can read it and help shed some light on the note" Mundale went on. Detective Mundale led them into an empty room next to Eva Tucker's room. "Mr. Rushton do you have any information that may help us in the investigation? He asked him, looking for some kind of a response from Cal to let him know something that he didn't know.

"If you mean do I know whose responsible for this, the answer is no" Cal told him, looking Mundale straight in the eyes.

Detective Mundale brought out the letter in the plastic bag, handing it to Cal to read. "This might give you some clues," Mundale said waiting to see Cal's reaction. Cal read the note while Amanda and Mundale stood silent. Cal's knees felt weak; his knees started to buckle. He felt a wave of thoughts enter his mind. Amanda grabbed a chair in the room sliding it to where he was. She took his arm helping him to sit before he collapsed. Mundale seemed shocked at the look in Cal's eyes.

Cal could see a man enter Eva's room. He watched the man put the pillow over Eva's face. She didn't struggle, she just stopped breathing, and Eva Tucker didn't even know the man was in her room. Cal couldn't see the mans face, only his back holding her down. The man let go of the pillow, turning to walk out of the room. The face of the man was vague. All Cal managed to make out was dark hair, mustache and a blank stare on his face. He felt himself slowly coming back out of his trance.

The note in the bag slipped out of his hand and fell to the floor. Mundale looked at him and then at Amanda.

"What's going on here?" Noticing Cal's trance like state.

"He will explain to you," she told Mundale, waiting for Cal to come out of the trance to see what he had learned. It took Cal a couple of minutes to get his bearings. This vision didn't take as much out of Cal as previous ones. The violence was mild the pain and terror weren't there as in previous visions.

Cal opened his eyes looking up at the detective. Mundale hovered above him waiting for an explanation. Mundale was confused by Cal's actions he watched Cal's strange expressions on his face.

"This note was left behind by the killer after he smothered Eva" Cal told him.

"Tell me something I don't know" Mundale said pulling over another chair in front of Cal's, waiting for more of an explanation.

Cal went on to explain to the detective about his visions, nightmares and dreams. He told Mundale about Colin Ray Barker participation in his visions. He went on to tell him about his near death experience and what had happened since then. He left out the money that was left and the keys to the car. He explained about the ear that was sent to him. He told Mundale that the killer wanted to be caught. The killer was making contact with him through his visions. He explained about Amanda's presence and that he feared for her life now.

He told Mundale that the killer could see his every move and now was waiting for the killer to make his next move but didn't know what it would be.

"You mentioned Colin Ray Barker" the detective interrupted.

"I arrested him for the death of Carmen Diago, his alleged girlfriend" the detective told him.

"His fingerprints were over the place, blood was found in his room which fit the DNA of Carmen Diago". "After he committed suicide in prison, the death's started again". The detective commented. "This note what can you tell me about it" he asked Cal.

Cal read the note again, held in front of him by Mundale.

"This note is telling you that he has killed ten times" Mundale paused

"He won't stop until he's caught". Cal said.

"I only know of three victims" Cal looked at Mundale, "I wish I could tell you more but I only see what he wants me to see".

"Eva makes six that I'm aware of" the detective muttered "Ten" he shook his head.

Mundale now knew there were four more victims that he was unaware of. He thought for a minute maybe the killer had moved here after his first few victims. Mundale sat thinking about the victims he knew. That meant there were four more victims. Maybe other victims would show up, if he checked out other cities. He would have to see if the same type of crimes were unsolved in other cities.

He had to get more information before the killer struck again. If he had to he would use Cal Rushton to help him catch the killer. The killer was trying to make contact with Cal that was evident by the evidence and Cal's statements.

"Maybe if I saw more evidence from other victims I could help you" Cal suggested.

CHAPTER VI
PIECE BY PIECE

Detective Mundale didn't believe in physics, but he had to follow any lead he could. Cal gave Mundale a brief description of the killer of Eva Tucker. Dark hair, tall and well built. Not much to go on, but at least that narrowed it down to being a white man.

"Would you be willing to take a polygraph?" Mundale asked him.

"Is he under suspicion?" Amanda spoke silent until now.

"I can tell you that I've been with Cal during Eva's death" she said trying to justify Cal's whereabouts.

"I assure you Miss Riley it's simply routine" the detective told her "I have to rule out every suspect that I can, this man has to be caught before he kills again" Mundale said his facial expressions serious and worried. "Would you be willing to work with another clairvoyant? The detective asked.

Cal agreed to work with Mundale if he made the evidence in

the other cases accessible to him. Mundale explained that he couldn't make those things accessible to him. Cal said that it might help to narrow down the killer if he could see them. Mundale agreed that it was a possibility that he might find something that Mundale did not see. They agreed and shook hands; Cal and Amanda left the room. Cal was curious to see if any more clues would show up if he looked at the other cases Mundale had access to.

"Meet me at my office 11:00am tomorrow morning" Mundale told Cal and Amanda on the way out the door.

It was 12am when they left the hospital to return to Cal's apartment. Amanda didn't want to stay alone; she was now afraid and frightened by all the events. She didn't know whether she could even sleep or not. She trusted Cal and believed in him. She was frightened but as long as he was with her she felt strangely safe. Back at the apartment Cal sat on the sofa. Amanda put one of his T-shirts on and prepared for bed. She came out of the washroom sitting beside Cal on the sofa.

"I'm scared," she confessed.

"I know" Cal said putting an arm around her. "I think tomorrow we should get a few things from your place" he suggested. "I think you should stay here until we figure out what's going on," he told her thinking about what had happened to Eva Tucker. "I think this is the safest place for you to be right now". Trying not to worry her.

Amanda laid her head on his shoulder, putting a hand on her chest.

"Can you sleep?" he asked her.

"I'm not sure, but could you sleep with me" she asked, she thought she would feel safer if he was right beside her.

"Are you sure?" Cal said kissing her on the forehead to comfort her.

"Please" she asked, squeezing him tighter.

They snuggled together drifting off to sleep.

It was strange thought Cal that he never imagined sleeping with a woman without thinking about sex, especially a woman as beautiful as Amanda.

Cal woke up at 6am; he slept the night without any nightmares. He woke up a couple of times during the night feeling Amanda lying beside him. He went to the kitchen turning the coffeepot on. He looked at the morning sky. It wasn't even dawn yet; the sky was just turning a faint gray. He noticed that it had finally stopped snowing. He smelled the coffee brewing. He made himself a cup of coffee. He noticed the Mercedes keys lying on the counter where he had left them. He wondered where this car was and if it belonged to someone. He sipped the coffee looking out the patio doors at the sunrise.

He held the keys to the car in his hand, noticing the alarm button on them. His finger pressed the alarm button on the chain. He heard the car alarm go off and saw the lights flashing in the parking lot of the apartment building. The alarm shocked him, he looked down at the keys he had put on the kitchen table.

"I'll be damned," Cal said scrambling to shut the alarm off, spilling hot coffee on him.

"Shit" he cursed out loud, dropping the cup onto the floor.

"What's wrong?" Amanda said coming from the bedroom still groggy from sleep.

"You won't believe this" Cal said calling her over to the patio doors.

He slid open the doors pressing the car starter as he did so. The car headlights came on, its engine purring. There in the parking lot sat the Mercedes. Cal had hit the car alarm on the key chain.

"Oh my God" Amanda said stunned by the sight of the car.

"I don't believe this" Cal muttered turning the engine off.

"I'll wait till it's fully daylight and I'll go see if there's anything in the car" Cal said hoping there might be a note of some kind.

He wondered how long the car had been there and if there was yet another clue to the killer left behind in the car. Amanda sat down on the sofa, she yawned and stretched. Cal poured her a cup of coffee bringing it too her.

"This might help," he said handing her the coffee.

Cal sat down beside her; she leaned over and kissed him on the lips.

"Thanks" she said simply.

"I should be thanking you, you're the only good thing that has come out of this mess," he said putting his arm around her to comfort her. He was still amazed that the Mercedes was sitting in the parking lot and wondered how long it had been there. Cal and Amanda found that they were falling in love. The circumstances were strange but they each knew what they were feeling towards each other. They sat waiting for the sun to come up fully, making small talk. They talked mostly about family, friends and relationships. Although, from completely different backgrounds they both felt drawn to know more about each other. Maybe, it was all the excitement, the mystery that was drawing them closer.

They waited another half-hour; finally Cal got up to go out to the strange car. He felt reluctant to go see what was next. He looked out the window at the parking lot below. The beautiful Burgundy, convertible sat there waiting for him to find the mystery inside. He put his boots on grabbing a coat on the way out the door.

"I'm almost scared to see what's in that car," Cal said going out the door.

"Want me to come with you?" she asked hesitantly.

"No, I think you better stay here" He said opening the door and locking it behind him.

Amanda went to the patio doors staring at the car below. What would he find in that car she wondered? Cal stepped outside the front doors into the chilly morning. It was cold but at least the sun seemed to be trying to break through. Cal thought for a second, here it was the last day of February, only a few weeks ago this all started. Since then his world has been full of so many weird things. What would be next, what was waiting for him in that car?

Cal neared the car, unlocking the car door as he did so. The black leather interior was gorgeous. Sure enough sitting on the passenger's seat was a brown envelope. The envelope was bulging with something inside. Cal reached into the glove box of the car. Inside the glove box were papers for the car. Maybe this would give him some idea where the car came from. He pulled them out startled to see his name on the registration. The insurance papers were the same, also in his name. Someone had managed to forge his name in the signature area. Whoever signed them knew his signature. He rifled through the rest of the papers in the dash. He found a receipt, payment for the car. It was paid fully by cash. He was hoping to find something to track the car, some kind of clue.

Cal saw the name on top of the receipt, Sanford's Mercedes, well that was a start. At least now he knew where the car had come from. He looked at the address of the dealership, Smith's Cove, nearly a three-hour drive away. Maybe the contents of the envelope would help him more.

He picked up the envelope getting out of the car. He scooped up the paperwork for the car taking them inside. He was still amazed that the person had taken the time to sign the car in his name. Leaving no trace to where it had come from. His mind wondered how someone would be able to purchase a car in his name and put all the papers in place in his name as well.

He looked back at the beautiful car, someone had a lot of money to throw away he told himself. Whoever was doing this was a wealthy individual there was no doubting that. He walked back inside the apartment being greeted by Amanda at the door.

"Did you look?" she said referring to the envelope.

"Not yet, but look at the paperwork" he said handing the papers to her.

He pulled out a chair at the kitchen table putting the envelope down on the table. He stared at the envelope unsure if he could open it. He was sure he would find more bizarre things in the envelope but what would he find? The envelope felt fairly heavy, it bulged with contents something rattled in the bottom of it. He hoped it wasn't another body part. Cal carefully broke the seal on the envelope, pulling out a file folder from inside. Then a letter with the words on it, "open me last". He shook the envelope, a set of keys falling out sliding across the table, the key chain immediately catching Amanda's eye. There were words around the outer edge. It was the strangest thing to see this key chain rattling across the kitchen table.

"The Devils brotherhood" she said "What's that mean?" she said recoiling her hand from the keys.

"Probably just another clue to this damn mystery" Cal said picking them up. Two keys dangled from the key chain. "I wonder what these are too?" Cal said puzzled.

On the front of the blood red folder were the words "Guess Who?'

Cal opened the cover of the folder; there in front of him was the beginning of the puzzle.

It was a newspaper column, the headline of a newspaper.

"Millionaire murders wife and daughter" he flipped the page.

"Scranton mistress of millionaire found slain" he turned to the next one.

"Another brutal sex slaying in bay area" the article read, turning to the next one. "Young couple found dead in bizarre sex crime" this one was mid west.

The clippings were all about the deaths of sex crimes. Cal got to the next article, which wasn't a headline, just a side column.

"Fox Creek Business Woman's body found," he read knowing it was Carmen Diago.

Then the next clipping "Senator plea for missing daughter"

Then the final clipping "Senator Logan vows to find killer"

Amanda read the columns now, she sat back flipping through each one of them looking for something to link them together.

This may be of some help," she said reading the columns.

"He's toying with me," Cal said holding the envelope in his hands unsure whether to open it or not.

Cal knew inside he would find another bizarre clue, but what? He opened the envelope, his hands shaking as he did so. There inside was another cryptic letter, another part of the strange puzzle.

"I know you can feel me"

"I know you see my evil"

"Are you clever enough to challenge me"

"Rich man, Poor man"

"No one is safe"

"Killing is easy"

"It's getting caught is the challenge"

Then the rest of the letter, which read: "If you read these clippings, pick up on the clues. Death is the key to finding me. I'll show you no mercy, torment your soul. Tease you with gifts, taunt you with clues. Another dead-end, another turn in the road. I know where you live; I'm watching you now. But, as I was once told, trust only yourself, for no one else cares. It's a world full of right's, a world full of wrongs. An unfaithful, unpredictable race. I've corrupted the rich, diseased the weak. Made the Godly unsure. Is it enough to do great things, when evil gives more pleasure? To take a life without challenge, destroy a soul. Fallen angel is what I am. I live on the dark side, taking only the weak. The tormented souls, the disillusioned in God. Now back to business, who will be next? For you see you are the only one to stop me, are you intelligent enough. The truth lies within your mind. Piece by piece you will see it's the mind of me that controls you. Do not contact the police, only you can solve this.

Guess who?

Cal crumpled up the paper in anger. His face was flushed, his heart raced. His hands were shaking with rage. "Who are you?" he roared in anger. He was shaken by what he was reading, this killer was challenging him, taunting him and leading him on.

Whoever he was, Cal was sure of one thing the man was a genius, and the fact remained he had to also be wealthy.

"Cal, it's okay honey," she said putting her arms around his neck.

"Why is he doing this?" Cal said putting his head between his hands.

"We have to be able to put this puzzle together," Amanda said indicating the clippings in the folder. "There has to be some clues in here that will lead us in the right direction.

They went through the clippings one by one. The first one had the number 2 circled in red markers, two victims the millionaire's wife and daughter. The article said the millionaire, Hank C. Crossling III came home to find them murdered, or so he claimed. The wife was raped and beaten beyond recognition. His daughter six years old was found in her bedroom. She was shot once in the head. The newspaper went on to say it took the jurors six hours to deliberate a guilty verdict, on Crossling. Crossling's powerful empire enabled him to get off on bail set at 5 million dollars.

Being free until the court could reach life or execution verdict. Cal flipped the next paper. Millionaire blamed for death of mistress. Again, Crossling had no concrete alibi and was found guilty. He was out on bail during her murder. He was sent to prison until sentencing for the first two deaths. He would then be prosecuted on the third murder. While in jail Crossling cracked under pressure, not sure if he could handle prison. He was institutionalized in an alyssum for the dangerous and mentally unstable. Sentencing was delayed again, but at least Crossling was behind bars. The papers never indicated what became of Crossling. Was he sentenced to death, life or worse spending the rest of his days in an institution?

The next article was a sex slaying in the Bay area. A woman's body was found brutally raped and murdered. The woman apparently was in her home at the time of the murder. Her body was found a few day's after the murder. She had been mutilated and raped. The woman was a student at the local university and was 22 years old. Family and friends had no clues to the murder and it was left unsolved.

The next clipping was the sex slaying of a young couple. Their land rover was found in a wooded area with two dead victims inside. The man had been shot once in the head, the woman was raped, tortured and murdered. The investigation had no leads on the crime. The two were on their way to a wedding and had stopped to rest.

Next clipping a woman has gone missing from her job as a waitress. She had been missing for four days. There wasn't much to do with her; just that she had disappeared. Her body was never found.

The next clipping, another young girl found missing. Asking the public for any information leading to the disappearance. The young girl a university student had gone missing after coming back late from friends. There was no information on her whereabouts.

Then the next two Carmen Diago, Kathleen Logan that made nine. Now of course Eva which made the tenth victim. But, of all the clippings Hank Crossling was the only one found guilty of charges of murder. "Cal did you notice the dates on these" Amanda said leafing through the clippings.

"No, why?" Cal asked his curiosity peaked.

"The first one is July 13th, 1975. The second October 13th, 1975 then February 13th, 1999. Twenty four years Cal" she sat stunned by the dates. "The next date is April 21, 1999, then September 10th 1999, Then it skips to August 21st 2002, then December 21st 2002. Then Carmen Diago January 12th 2004, Kathleen December 15th 2004. Now Eva, is the last" Amanda said reaching each date out loud.

"Are you sure about those dates?" Cal sat amazed.

"Yes Cal 24 years between the first three deaths and the rest" she said shuffling the clippings again to make sure she was right.

"But why, that's unbelievable" Cal sat looking through the clippings. "We have to meet with Detective Mundale this morning" Cal said looking at the time.

Cal sat leafing through the clippings again. The name Hank Crossling could be his first clue. He had to find out where the man was and if he was still alive. That was along time ago when the crimes started. The man claimed to have been not guilty, but was he the one still alive out there somewhere doing the killings. After all he was wealthy, as the papers had indicated. He kept flipping the man's name over and over in his mind; something was familiar with either the story or the name.

Detective Mundale sat at his desk looking at files from the forensics reports. The DNA tests, the letter that the killer had left and whatever information gathered at the crime scene. He wondered if Rushton's bizarre tale was just a tale. There were no fingerprints, no motives to kill Eva Tucker.

He flipped open the file folder on his desk. The information he had on the murder victims in the land rover. That's when the case was passed to him. The other folders were Carmen Diago and Kathleen Logan and now Eva Tucker. What was it that had his killer contacting Cal?

Rushton? Did Rushton know him or had he set the murders up himself. But, Rushton had no motives; he had alibis. Rushton wasn't the killer, but he may lead him to the killer.

Mundale's world was turning upside down in a hurry. Long hours on the case, lack of sleep and not eating properly were making him tired. His wife was getting agitated with him, telling him that he was possessed with his work and didn't care about her or his children. He had to give Rushton a polygraph. He knew that this didn't prove anything even if Rushton failed. However, he had to be sure that Rushton was telling him the truth, beyond a shadow of doubt. He also had Dr. Watson who specialized in clairvoyant and physic behaviors. The Doctor was coming to the office to meet with him and Rushton.

He looked at the method of killing; the same brutality was used on each victim. The man in the truck was shot in the head once, execution style. Eva Tucker was raped and beaten, but she survived. The killer had let her live to send a message, apparently to Cal Rushton. Mundale wasn't convinced that there was only one killer. Maybe, Rushton was an accomplice in these murders. He shook his head; he was really grasping for straws now. The only thing he did know was a killer was out there somewhere. If the media got a hold of this news, with the rumor of a serial murderer, the town would be in crisis. He didn't need FBI agents and city officials screaming serial killer. Mundale cringed at the thought of a serial killer stalking his streets. What made a serial killer the serial killer? The facts that the murders were the same in many aspects. The fact was murder was murder, be it one or ten. Mundale lit a cigarette inhaling the blue smoke. A knock came on the door.

"Enter" Mundale said leaning back in his chair.

"Dr. Watson to see you sir" the young officer announced.

"Show him in" He said taking another puff off the cigarette.

Dr. Sam Watson came into the room carrying a brief case. The overweight man puffed as he took a seat across from Mundale. He sat down opening the briefcase he held on his lap.

"Thought you quit those thing" Watson said waving a hand to clear the smoke.

"Shut up Sam" Mundale said smiling at the overweight man.

"I see your still a moody bastard" Dr. Watson snickered, getting a dig in on Mundale.

"Only with you Sam" Mundale said sliding the files across the table.

"What have we got here?" The Dr. said pulling a pair of glasses out of his pocket.

Mundale and Watson had worked together on other cases. Only when the need arose did Mundale think of Watson. When all the other obstacles were covered and Mundale could think of nothing else, then and only then did he call Watson.

Mundale figured any kind of lead was better than nothing. They had become friends over the years and he had seen Watson help solve other cases.

"Same case, new victims, new faces, same damn story" Mundale said butting out his cigarette.

Mundale went on to brief the Dr. on the case. Watson was familiar with the case having tried to help when Colin Ray Barker was charged with murder. Mundale told Watson about Cal and his visions. He explained about Eva Tucker's death and the note written by the killer. Watson sat silently looking at the note, files and evidence. He said nothing waiting for Mundale to finish his story. Mundale told him that he wanted him to meet with Rushton. He thought maybe he could help unravel the dreams, nightmares and visions Rushton was having.

Mundale told Watson that this killer had claimed ten victims so far. Watson's eyes lit with the prospect of working on the case again. He knew that some of the victims were those that he had worked on with the disappearance of the two campers. They never did get any substantial lead on that case, although Watson told Mundale at the time that this wasn't the first time this killer had struck.

"Should I say the word?" Watson said looking squarely at Mundale.

"Don't get started on that again," Mundale warned.

"Barker told us there was a serial killer on the loose and we didn't believe him" Watson said leaning forward "You didn't believe him at the time and now it seems our serial killer has struck again.

"I told you Barker was the wrong man" Watson said his voice having resentment in it.

"The jury found him guilty, I just arrested him on the evidence given to me" Mundale argued.

"So this Rushton, how long has he been a clairvoyant" Watson asked, trying to find out information on Rushton before the meeting.

Mundale went on to tell him about the things that Rushton had told him. He told Watson the story as told by Rushton. He then asked Watson if he could tell if Rushton was lying or telling the truth about being a clairvoyant. Watson commented that sometimes a traumatic event in someone's life could bring on such instances. He also said that once diagnosed as a Clairvoyant that its possible Cal had the gift but didn't realize until what happened to him. Watson was interested in meeting Cal Rushton. Maybe, then he could put to rest the fact that Colin Ray Barker was sent to prison on a wrongful conviction.

Mundale then told Watson that Cal Rushton had claimed that the killer had killed ten times. Watson was astounded by the claim of ten kills. Watson's own experience with clairvoyant and paranormal dealings was limited. He was more of an expert on the science rather than the actual experience. The knock came on the door ending their conversation.

"Cal Rushton and Amanda Riley are here to see you sir," the same young officer announced.

"Take them down to the interview room" Mundale responded, giving him some more time to brief Watson on what was going on.

Cal Rushton sat anxiously taking hold of Amanda Riley's hand. He brought along the file of clippings as well as the letter.

Cal thought that also coming clean on the gifts would be a good idea. But, Amanda disagreed telling him she thought that it might make him look guilty. Cal agreed that it would be a good idea that maybe he might be held responsible for withholding evidence. In the end they decided to wait until the outcome of the meeting was over before discussing it further.

Detective Mundale came into the room followed by Dr. Watson. Cal thought that Watson was here to give him a polygraph. But, in reality he wanted to see if he could get anything from Cal.

"Good morning Mr. Rushton, Miss Riley" Detective Mundale said.

"This is Dr. Sam Watson he will be here to join in the interview" Mundale paused.

"Do you object to Dr. Watson asking some questions?" he asked, looking at Cal and then Amanda.

"No, not at all, the sooner I find out some things the better" Cal told him, trying to find out as much as he could himself as well.

Cal slid the file across the table to detective Mundale. Mundale paused for a minute then flipped the file open. He was shocked by what was inside the file.

"What's this?" Mundale asked confusion on his face.

Another message from the killer" Cal said sitting back getting ready for a barrage of questions.

Mundale opened the folder his eyes wide as he started looking at the clippings.

"Jesus" me muttered scanning through them.

He passed them over to Dr. Watson as he started reading the letter. Mundale noticed that the paper was wrinkled and creased.

"When did you get this?" Mundale asked.

"This morning in my car" Cal told him, not telling him about the Mercedes.

"In your car?" Watson interrupted, how would anyone have access to his vehicle he was thinking.

"I don't lock my car never have" Cal said ready for more questions.

"Did you notice the dates on those clippings" Cal added indicating as far back as they went.

Mundale re-read the letter, while Watson read the clippings checking the dates.

"There's a twenty five year span in here" Watson said confused "Do you mean to say this same son of a bitch has been doing this for that long without getting caught".

"This is one sick son of a bitch," Mundale said passing the letter to Watson.

Mundale and Watson had been working on this case together since the arrest of Colin Ray Barker. Mundale didn't believe in clairvoyance or the Para-normal. Then Barker had started rambling on about seeing things. Mundale was still convinced that Barker was just covering up for the death of Carmen Diago. Barker's defense requested that an expert on clairvoyance be called in. Enter Dr. Watson, to see if he could understand and clarify Colin Ray Barker's story. Dr. Watson believed Colin Ray Barker saw something but couldn't persuade Mundale. The judge and jury in the trial were convinced also that Colin Ray Barker was guilty. Nearly a year passed without another death, while Barker was in prison. Detective Mundale was satisfied that the right man was behind bars. Dr. Watson was second-guessing himself thinking maybe Mundale was right after all. That was until the death of Kathleen Logan. Detective Mundale was shocked that another gruesome murder had taken place. To top it off a well know politician's daughter. It was the killer's mark to tell the law and judicial system they had the wrong man.

Dr. Watson started the interview with Cal Rushton. He asked him questions about the murders and the visions he was having. Dr. Watson went on to tell Cal that since his traumatic experience had happened he was given a gift. Cal told Watson it wasn't a gift it was more of a curse. Dr. Watson asked him if he tried to have a vision, could he. Cal told him that they happen spontaneously.

"Would you like to try?" Watson asked as Mundale sat listening.

Mundale was still skeptical about the whole thing but in the end what did he have to lose even if it was one minor clue that was not found.

"I don't think it will work" Cal told him, not sure if he could see anything while being tensed up like he was.

"Would you mind if I hypnotized you?" Watson asked him "That may relax you enough so that we can see if there is anything you can tell us".

"If it removes any suspicion for me, I'll try anything" Cal said leaning back again.

Watson proceeded to try and hypnotize Cal. Amanda Riley was escorted out of the room so she didn't have to witness it. It took nearly twenty minutes and three tries before Watson succeeded in hypnotizing Cal. Mundale sat back mildly amused at the stuff they were trying. The doctor preceded taking Cal's hand in his.

"Cal these dreams you're having can you explain them to me"

In that instant the vision came, it was sudden and violent. Detective Mundale started to get up thinking the whole idea was absurd. He noticed the color drain from Dr. Watson's face.

Dr. Watson had a look of shock and terror on his face. Cal was into a vision of Kathleen Logan's murder. The breaking of her ribs, cracking of her jaw. Watson began to tremble his face filled with perspiration. Beads of sweat running off the big man's face. Cal's fist clenched Dr. Watson's hand tighter. Dr. Watson breathing rapidly increased, his heart was pounding in his chest. Dr. Watson broke the grip of Cal Rushton toppling over backwards onto the floor. The once white face of Dr. Watson now turned purple. He was having a heart attack, and serious trouble breathing. His eyes rolled back in his head, Mundale couldn't believe what he was seeing.

"Fuck sakes" Mundale retorted running for the door for help.

Detective Mundales shouted orders for someone to call an ambulance. Watson's eyes rolled back in his head. Cal sat in the chair his heart racing now out of the trance broken by Watson's fall to the floor. He had shared his vision with Watson and now the big man was having a heart attack right before his eyes. Mundale squatted beside Watson's side trying to give the man CPR.

"Hang in there Sam, helps on the way" Mundale said looking into the horrified eyes of Sam Watson. He was still conscious and trying to speak to Mundale. The detective leaned down putting his ear next to the big man's mouth. Watson had seen what Rushton was able to see all along; in the process it had given him a heart attack. Mundale leaned over Sam Watson horrified trying to give the man CPR until the paramedics arrived.

"I saw it Jim," the big man said before he fell into unconsciousness.

Paramedics arrived on the scene successfully reviving the almost dead Dr. Watson. His heart couldn't take the stress, and terror he had seen in the vision shown to him by Cal Rushton. The big man had a massive heart attack; he regained consciousness briefly on his trip to the hospital. He couldn't imagine the experience he had witnessed. Kathleen Logan's struggle to survive, the horror the young woman had suffered. He would recover but he realized that once and for all what he had studied and practiced was more real than ever before. He would slip into a coma and never get the chance to tell Detective Mundale the details that would still be a mystery to everyone accept him and Cal Rushton.

Cal Rushton was drained; his mind and emotions were starting to deteriorate with the visions and nightmares. He sat soaked in perspiration watching the paramedics work on Sam Watson. He knew at least someone else saw his visions and nightmares, and they weren't his imagination. Others said they believed him, but they didn't experience what he was seeing and feeling.

Detective Mundale sat down in a chair across from Cal. Amanda came back into the room pulling a chair up beside Cal. He had a blank stare on his face, one of disbelief. He had no choice but to accept Cal Rushton's visions now.

Dr. Watson had mumbled that he had seen them. No words were spoken for several minutes. Each person in the interview room sat absorbed in their own thoughts. It was Amanda who finally broke the silence.

"What happens next?" Amanda asked detective Mundale.

"We try to find the man responsible for all these deaths" He said picking up the folder and the clippings. "The bastard is out there somewhere and God knows when he will strike again"

"I have to have these Cal" Mundale said referring to the clippings and letter.

"I would like copies, if that's okay with you" Cal said trying to piece things together in his mind.

"Are you willing to work with me to solve this thing?" Mundale asked him, hoping he would give full cooperation. "This is a police matter after all," Mundale continued.

"I think that's fair, don't you Cal" Amanda said putting her hand back into his.

Cal Rushton was exhausted and agreed to work with the detective on the case. They decided the best place to start would be the beginning, 1975. They would check the whereabouts of Hank Crossling, the wealthy millionaire. There was some doubt that he was still even alive. Detective Mundale would make a call to Hammond penitentiary. Hank Crossling would be there that's if he was still alive. In 1975 Crossling was 46 years old that means he would be 74 now. It was reported that after spending sometime in a phys ward that Crossling was returned to Hammond Penitentiary in 1989. That would be the place to start.

Amanda re-reads the newspaper clipping on Hank Crossling. He pled innocent in all three-murder charges. His enormous wealth made it impossible for to have an impartial trial. The three consecutive life sentences terms totaled 75 years. Beyond that there wasn't about the man himself.

To find that out they would have to dig into Crossling's past. Was this just another dead end? Did they have time to stop all the murders that was going on? This man had threatened to not stop until he was dead or caught. A question now entered Cal Rushton's mind. What was the Devil's Brotherhood? The key chain to this new set of keys had the Devil's Brotherhood on it. Was this just some sort of joke or was there really such an organization. If so what and who were they.

The thought of Dr. Watson's seeing the vision entered his mind.

Watson was supposedly an expert in psychic abilities. Did Watson survive his massive heart attack, Cal didn't know that yet. Detective Mundale asked Amanda and Cal to come into his office and wait while he made some phone calls. One of the young officers brought in some coffee for them while they waited. Mundale's first call was to the hospital to find out the condition on Sam Watson. The nurse told him that he was in critical condition but that he was stable. He remembered what the last thing Sam had said was "I saw him Jim" referring to Cal's shared vision.

Mundale knew he had a lot of work to do. He became fairly close with Sam Watson over the brief time they had known each other. He felt sorry for his family that's if he had one Mundale thought. He had never mentioned family to him. Mundale made his second call to the Hammond Penitentiary. It was located on a small south coast town near San Beradino, California. The warden offered to fax some information on Crossling to give him a lead on living relatives. So Crossling had passed away, now he knew that. He also told him he would give him a list of all the visitors and relatives that came to visit him in prison.

Mundale waited by the fax machine, checking in to tell Cal and Amanda about Dr. Watson. He lit another cigarette and gulped down a cup of coffee while he waited. Cal was shocked that Dr. Watson was in that serious of a condition. He felt the blame for sharing his vision with him. Of course he didn't think it possible to share visions like they did. How was he to know it would almost kill the man?

Amanda sat silent looking at the folder of the clippings. She read each one searching for some clue or something that would draw the murders together. She was still nervous about the whole bizarre nightmare.

Detective Mundale came back into the office carrying papers faxed to him. The covering page had a picture of Crossling with all his convictions and his identification record. There were documents on Crosslings relatives and visitors.

Crossling had died in prison in 1996 from complications of pneumonia. He was 68 at the time. Next, was a copy of Crosslings worksheet while in prison? Hammond was a small maximum-security prison, which housed 650 inmates. Crossling had been a model prisoner, helping organize the work teams and other things. To his dying day Crossling had never admitted to the murders he was convicted of. Instead he stood by his claim that he was innocent. Crossling was due for parole hearing in June 1997. He never got the chance having died before ever witnessing freedom again.

The enormous wealth Crossling had on the outside did benefit him in prison to a certain extent. He was able to invest some of his money, through lawyers to make Hammond State Penitentiary's library. Also he helped with a video and music library for the inmates. He also helped with the families of prisoners that had children. In prison Crossling could do no wrong with the other prisoners, guards and even the warden. Detective Mundale had the opportunity to speak with the warden of Hammond Penitentiary. He asked if there were ever any problems while Crossling was in prison.

The only thing Crossling had done was allegations from another inmate. The inmate was a loner in the prison system. He was irate that Crossling claimed to have organized a group of the other inmates to start some kind of club. The man dropped the allegations a short while later. Crossling and him became best friends after that, until the man was released in April 1993.

Mundale wanted to know the man's whereabouts, call it a hunch but he had to follow up. The man's name was John

Natas. The last the warden heard Natas had moved east. Natas did his time on the inside and never caused any more problems on the outside world again. He finished his work with the parole officer and was allowed to move back east. The last time anyone had heard from Natas, was June 1989. Mundale had a strange feeling about Natas. Did he have anything to do with the murders? Was Natas the model citizen that everyone believed him to be? How old was Natas now he said. The warden told him he was 44 when he was released, so that made him 55 now.

Mundale informed Cal about the information he had received. He discussed with Cal whether he thought they were wasting their time on Crossling. Cal didn't think Crossling had anything to do with the murders. But, he did admit that maybe Natas was responsible. The strange club inside the prison intrigued Mundale. Mundale wasn't sure if the club still existed or if it was just smoke and mirrors. No matter Mundale decided to take a trip to Hammond penitentiary.

Detective Mundale would go see the warden and dig up any information and maybe interview some of the inmates that knew Natas when he was there. Hammond Penitentiary sounded like it might have some leads for Mundale to follow up.

Cal and Amanda decided they would do research on the Internet library, try to find the whereabouts of John Natas. Things were getting confusing with Crossling and now Natas entering the picture. One thing Cal knew Crossling had money to burn. Now, Cal was receiving gifts of money, new car and of course the keys that he wasn't sure what they belonged to. Amanda and Cal decided to go back to Amanda's. She had a computer and he needed a change of venues. Cal stopped off at his apartment for clean clothes and personal effects. Cal also took along 2000.00 of the money. He thought he might need it for the killers next move.

Cal decided to follow Amanda to her apartment driving the new Mercedes. In the case that they would need two cars Cal let Amanda drive the 71' Camaro. He had never let anyone drive his car except his brother Bobby. Pulling into the parking lot Amanda had a brainstorm.

She came running back to where he was parking.

"I wonder if there's anything in the trunk," she said indicating the Mercedes.

"Good idea, why do you always think of these things" he smiled at her popping the trunk button.

The trunk flipped open with Amanda standing by the back of the car. Cal could see the look of puzzle on her face as he got out of the car. She didn't say anything, she just looked dumb founded. Cal went and stood besides her peering into the trunk. In the trunk were two suitcases. One with Cal's name on it the other with Amanda's. Now Cal knew that whoever it was knew about Amanda even down to her last name. What were the suitcases for and why were they stashed inside the trunk of the car.

"What's this" Cal said tugging at the suitcases.

The suitcases were light or had nothing except some bizarre notes. Cal read the notes out loud looking at the two suitcases in amazement.

"Better wait to get them inside" Cal suggested lifting the bags out of the trunk. They carried them back into Amanda's apartment. They sat the bags down looking at each other wondering who was going to open them.

"Which one first" Cal said scared to see what was inside.

"I don't know but, you open them both" she said raising her arms in the air.

Cal cautiously lifted the bag with Amanda's name on it onto the kitchen table. Amanda cringed at the sound of the zipper. She stood back not want to see, but curious enough to try to sneak a peek. Inside Amanda's bag was a bikini, lingerie and sun tan lotion. As well there was a note under the lingerie.

"The unexpected sometimes, is not what you expect. I think you'll find these things to your taste. Looking forward to meeting you in the near future. You can't always judge a book by its cover".

"Swim wear and sleep wear," Cal said waving Amanda over closer to look.

"Okay, now mine" Cal said picking his up hoping that his didn't hold some kind of crazy puzzle or body part. Amanda was still cautious of the other suitcase. Cal's was a bit heavier as he plunked it down on the table. Inside the one with his name was a bottle of champagne. A pair of shorts, a Hawaiian shirt, a camera and two plane tickets and a hotel confirmation. "Miami, Florida" Cal said a stunned look on his face.

"There's a note here Cal" Amanda said lifting up the clothing.

"How clever are you Cal? Are you clever enough to figure out where this began. The brotherhood is watching and waiting for you. God's world is paved with good intentions. Our world is paved with others good intentions. By the time you read this another victim has been claimed. This victim is not like the rest. This victim may live or may die, it depends on you. Even though I'm near, I'm also far away instead of waiting Cal, I've decided the time has come. No police. It will be you and me and our minds. I'm Waiting Cal, so is the victim. Hurry before I steal another soul. Number eleven is a slip of the blade a turn of the knife, or a slow torture away. You see through my eyes, I see through yours. Isn't it time to find out why, who and where all this will end Guess who?

CHAPTER VII
BROTHERHOOD BEGINNINGS

Detective Mundale arrived at the Hammond penitentiary. He was escorted to Warden Sims office. Warden Sims a short plump man sat behind his desk with an open file in front of him. He had a balding head and wore his glasses down on his nose so he could look over them when speaking to someone. Sims had warden of the penitentiary for along time and was a no bullshit type of warden. He didn't tolerate disobedience from any of the inmates and liked to control all the situations regarding prisons and guards.

"Detective Mundale" the warden stood up extending his hand.

"Have a seat" he paused "I trust your flight was good," the warden said sitting back down. He looked over at Mundale and offered him a cigar.

Warden Sims didn't tolerate any unnecessary foolishness. He was direct and to the point. In front of him was the original file of Hank Crossling. He told Mundale the same thing they had discussed earlier. Mundale mentioned the Devils Brotherhood to the warden. He could see the color drain from his face and sense the tension in the air. The Warden's personality changed, immediately denying it as nonsense.

"The Devil's Brotherhood, that's a ridiculous rumor" he denied.

"Your information is strained at best detective. There is none, nor was there ever any such organization in this facility". He paused his tone of voice seemed angrier. "If you've wasted your time coming here on that, then your wasting my time as well as yours," The warden said sternly fidgeting with his hands. "Unless you have something else to add, then I'm afraid I have other business to attend to". The warden sat eyes getting bigger.

Mundale could tell by the reaction that there was something to the allegations of "The Devil's Brotherhood", when he mentioned the word he could sense the tension and strain in Warden Sims.

"I'm sorry if I've offended you Warden, I thought it was all nonsense as well," Mundale said trying to smooth things over.

The warden accepted Mundale's apology asking if he would like a coffee. While they sat there comparing notes on Crossling another guard came in and brought in coffee.

"I'm sorry if I jumped down your throat earlier" the warden apologized.

"Was there anyone else that Crossling made friends with in here?" Mundale pried.

The warden sat for a moment, thinking about the other inmates.

"There is old Tom" the Warden answered, "He and Crossling were pretty close" the warden paused.

"Would it be possible to speak to him" Mundale asked hoping the warden would accommodate him.

"I don't see why not," the Warden said picking up the phone.

Mundale sat and had coffee with the Warden. They discussed Crosslings attitude while in prison. They also talked about whether he believed Crossling to be guilty of the crimes he was convicted of. The Warden made the response that he wasn't judge and jury he was just the innkeeper.

Mundale thanked him for his time before being escorted down to the visitors lobby to meet old Tom. Detective Mundale sat waiting for the prisoner to come to the visitors lobby. Warden Sims sudden brash and abrasive attitude change confused him. Mundale was convinced that this Devils Brotherhood did exist at one time. He was hoping for the same kind of clue when old Tom was escorted to his table. Old Tom sat down. He was completely snow white, his hair looked very unkempt. His hands were gnarled and covered with age spots. The old man's eyes fixed on Mundale. He looked nervous looking around his shoulder to see if he was being watched.

The guard stood back "Five minutes Tom".

The old man nodded his approval. He sat and crossed his hands looking at Mundale. He couldn't figure out who Mundale was and what he would want with him.

"Hi Tom" Mundale said sticking out his hand as a gesture.

"No contact" the guard said stepping forward.

Old Tom recoiled and sat looking straight-ahead not saying anything. It seemed to Mundale that old Tom hadn't any visitors in a long time and obviously wanted to know what Mundale would want with him.

"I'm detective Mundale," he said trying to get a response.

The old man didn't flinch he sat with his hands neatly folded on the table, staring blankly.

Mundale sat for 10 seconds wondering what to ask. Tom never said a thing as if he couldn't speak at all. Finally, Mundale had to ask the question.

"Have you heard of the Devil's Brotherhood," he asked point blank.

The old man's eyes widened, he looked slowly rolling one of his arms over. On the arm was the tattoo, the same one that Colin Ray Barker had. The circular tattoo, the outside ring said Devil's Brotherhood. Each letter spaced with an asterisk between them. In the center of the tattoo the number 804.

The old man's response was just as Mundale had suspected the Devils Brotherhood was for real. But, why was he so terrified when Mundale mentioned it and why did Warden Sims attitude change completely when Mundale mentioned the Devils Brotherhood.

"Are you a member?" Mundale questioned.

The old man nodded ever so slightly. He took another look over his shoulder seeing if the guard or anyone else was watching him. He seemed very nervous to Mundale.

"Okay did you know Hank Crosslings friends and family?" he paused "Did he ever mention them to you". He asked, prying for information on Crossling.

Mundale felt he was onto something but had no evidence yet. Detective Mundale sensed the extreme nervousness of Old Tom. The old man's eyes were twitching. He knew if he ever needed the old man to talk he would have to get him alone or with a court order. The old man looked weak and fragile. A good strong gust of wind would probably topple him over.

"Did you know Crosslings friend that was released in 1989, John Natas?" he asked.

Mundale was almost whispering now to help the old man feel more at ease with the questioning. The old man again nodded, a glimmer of a smile on his wrinkled face.

"That number on your arm, what does it mean?" Mundale asked him, curious if it had any kind of hidden meaning.

He whispered very lowly "number of murders" the old mans eyebrows raised.

Mundale nearly fell off his chair at Old Tom's response. Did he mean by him or by the members.

"You mean by the members?" Mundale whispered.

The old man only nodded again this time. He knew a lot but was unable to speak, he had probably been threatened to not speak of it, Mundale thought. It was strange that the old man knew so much yet could not say anything.

"One Minute" the guard bellowed looking at the clock.

"Would you talk if I got you transferred from here? Mundale questioned. The old man's eyes widened, the guard making his way by his side. The old man nodded his approval being led out of the room. The old man glanced back his eyes almost pleading for Mundale to do as he said. Mundale sat for a couple minutes trying to absorb what he just heard. The Devil's Brotherhood was an organization, he was positive with Old Tom's nods.

He left the room being greeted by Warden Sims near the door. He had to get Tom transferred if at all possible, and then maybe he could get the full story. He wouldn't be able to get the Warden to agree to it that was evident.

"Tom able to tell you anything?" The Warden asked his eyes narrowing.

"No, he didn't even speak, wouldn't answer anything I asked him" Mundale said a look of frustration on his face.

"Sorry didn't' figure he would be much good, but was worth a try" the Warden said looking suddenly very relaxed.

Cal Rushton finished packing his suitcase. He jammed it full of clothes. Amanda was still at her apartment also packing. The two had decided to give it a try. Cal put a call through to detective Mundale but only got told that the detective was away on business. Cal knew Mundale was in Hammond. He asked for the detectives voice mail. Leaving a message that he would be in touch. The trip wouldn't be pleasurable; he knew it would be all business. He realized that he had a limited amount of time before the killer struck again. Cal knew he had nothing to go on, but he knew the killer would contact him.

Cal and Amanda reached the airport, with Amanda having second thoughts about the trip. She told Cal her concerns; he told her maybe she should go somewhere else for a while, until the smoke cleared. Maybe friends or relatives would be a good idea until he figured things out. But, she argued that the killer knew her too. He knew where she lived; he had even been there with Kathleen. The two finally boarded the flight, each vowing to be silent about the events that had taken place.

Once the flight landed in Miami, they got a taxi to the Hilton Hotel. Under different circumstances the trip would have been quite enjoyable, but under the extreme conditions they were traveling it was un-nerving. Once at the reception desk they asked how long they would be staying. Cal asked how long there room was booked for. Two weeks was the response. The bellboy showed them to their room on the top floor over looking the lights of Miami.

The room amazed them, it just wasn't an ordinary room, and it was the honeymoon suite. The room had a heart shaped bed in the bedroom. The living room had a beautiful view of the city. The living room sunk down four steps to get to another landing where a hot tub sat by the patio doors overlooking the city. Amanda talked about how beautiful the room was as Cal started unpacking his suitcase. Cal brought all the money, and put it in bundles neatly to one side of the nightstand. He didn't know what was in store for either one of them so he came prepared for the worst.

"We may need it" Cal said referring to the money.

"I'll sleep in the living room," Cal said picking up a pair of faded Levi's to get changed.

"Cal" she said touching his shoulder.

Cal turned around kissing her passionately for the first time. Neither of them spoke as they undressed each other. Cal scooped her up in his arms, laying her on the bed. The passion and desire they felt for each other finally erupted. They lay on the bed looking into each other's eyes. Cal caressed her face with his hand, rubbing a finger over her lips.

"God your beautiful" He told her kissing her.

The two made love, each feeling something they had been looking for a very long time. They drifted off to sleep in each other's arms. Cal knew he had never felt like this before. He could only imagine a lifetime with her now. Amanda fell asleep first, Cal kissing her watching her sleep. Finally he fell into a deep sleep. A deep dark nightmare, within him…

Detective Mundale made a few phone call's to his connections seeing what the possibility of getting Tom Keene moved from Hammond to a minimum security prison. First he had to find out what Tom was in prison for. Murder, he knew but how many years and how long did he already serve. He called a friend in corrections to see what Tom Keene's crimes had been. Keene was arrested for the murder of two teenage girls in 1968. He was 45 at the time; apparently, the girls were making fun of his retarded son when he went crazy. He beat them to death with a shovel from the back of his pick up truck. He confessed to the murders and was sentenced to 50 years with no chance of parole.

Tom Keene would never see freedom again, although, now the sickly old man was harmless. Detective Mundale had a friend in a judge that he called next. Mundale went over the details with the judge asking if he could get the old man transferred. The Judge told Mundale it might take some time to get through the red tape. In meantime he could have some papers drawn up to have the man removed and put into a psychiatric hospital, until the paperwork was done. That was the best that the judge could do under the circumstances. Mundale agreed that it would be a start. At least the old man would be safe in the confines of a mental institution.

Mundale sat in his motel room going through what he had learned so far. It wasn't much but at least he knew the Devil's Brotherhood existed. But, Tom Keene might be to scare to talk or worse he may be already insane. He decided to check with the office to see if there were any messages. He was put through to his voice mail.

The first message was his wife. She had enough of their rocky relationship and was leaving with the kids to go back to New Hampshire with her parents. She said maybe they needed sometime apart until he got his priorities straight.

The next was the message left by Cal Rushton. The message was to the point and short.

"Detective Mundale, this is Cal Rushton calling. I've gotten another message from the killer. He wants me to fly to Miami; he left keys, reservations and two plane tickets to Miami. He said time was running out until victim #11. You can reach me at 1-955-555-1301 at the Hilton Hotel, room 1616. I'll expect you to call.

Mundale wasn't pleased, he didn't need Rushton going off

by his self and endangering his and Miss Riley's lives. He swore under his breath. He knew he had to follow his lead. Now, he had lost his wife and kids, he had two of his informants on the case in a chase in Miami. He was waiting to hear back form the judge on Tom Keene.

The phone rang breaking his concentration. He was hoping it would be the Judge to have Keane moved out of Hammond. That way he could at least get to speak with him.

"Mundale here" he answered.

"Detective Mundale, its Judge Munro here" he paused "We can get Tom

Keene into the state mental institution, but back in Lincoln, two hours from Hammond" the judge responded.

"How soon?" Mundale questioned, knowing the sooner the better before Warden Sims or someone else got to him.

"Well, Warden Sims lost it when I called him" the judge told him.

"He wanted to know if you put me up to this" the judge told Mundale.

"Fuck, I hope you told him no" Mundale said worried about the old man's life.

"I gave him a bullshit story about his case was under review by a social worker, because of his age," the judge said continuing. " But, I don't think he bought it" Judge Munro said.

"What's this all about anyway Jim?" the judge said.

"Have you ever heard of the Devil's Brotherhood?" Mundale asked the judge.

"That's an old story, thought that story died quite a few years ago," the judge said referring to the Brotherhood.

"I think it still exists and Tom Keene might help me prove it" Mundale told him.

The judge and Mundale finished their conversation. With

Judge Munro promising he would try to get Tom Keene transferred as soon as possible.

The judge still insisted that there was no Brotherhood, it was just a hoax started by someone's vivid imagination. He said he had heard the rumors of the Devils Brotherhood for years and thought it didn't exist since the 70's. However, he said anything is possible, and if still does exist I don't think too many people are aware of it. Detective Mundale knew that if Tom Keene knew anything he wouldn't speak where he was at now. But, away from Hammond penitentiary he may tell all. In the meantime someone might hurt the old man or even kill him.

Cal's nightmare that night was an experience that woke him from his sleep. Cal dreamt of the day he tried to commit suicide. This time he was being forced to kill himself. The man was huge and laughed at Cal on the chair hanging him. Cal begged for his life, telling the man in the mask he wanted to live. The masked man kicked the chair from under Cal. He swung from the rope struggling to free himself. He felt the life draining out of his body. He saw the mocking faces laughing at him.

Then he saw the faces of victims pleading for their lives. Kathleen Logan, Carmen Diago and Eva Tucker all were there. Eva's asked why he let her die. She begged for Cal to save her. Tears rolled down her face. Cal woke up with such a start. Amanda sat up beside him. He couldn't breath, his heart felt like it was being torn from his chest. The bed was soaked from Cal's sweat. He sat wide-eyed; Amanda trying to tell him it was only a nightmare. This one of the worst episodes yet, he contributed it to the fact that he was so close to finding out or close to the actual killer.

"It's okay' she kept repeating rubbing his back.

"Oh, my God" Cal said running his hands through his hair.

Tears came pouring down Cal's face he didn't know if he could go on any longer with these nightmares. Amanda tried her best to comfort him. The clock said 430am, Cal jumped out of bed. He went to the patio window overlooking the city of Miami. He stared out wondering why this was happening to him. He didn't want this gift or curse whatever it was any more. It wanted nothing more than to rid him of these dreams and visions.

"He's out there somewhere, waiting, watching" he told Amanda.

"We'll find him and catch him," she said standing beside him looking out the window with him.

"It's his move now" Cal said, "He knows the next step".

They decided to stay up and get and early start on the day. They showered, changed and went down to the hotel restaurant for breakfast. They ate their breakfast talking about what they had to do next.

Cal got curious to wondering if anyone had left any messages at the front desk for him. He went to the front desk clerk asking if there were any messages left for him. The desk clerk checked there is a letter left here for you Mr. Rushton. Cal got the letter, his heartbeat faster. He felt dizzy at the thought of opening the letter. He took the letter back into the dining room sitting down with Amanda. She looked at him a worried look on her face.

"I'm not sure I want to open this" he looked at her, his hands trembling.

She said nothing, but the color drained out of her face. She could tell that whatever it was bothering him was only getting worse now. With each passing day there seemed to be more and more. She hoped that this would end soon before it drove him insane. He ripped it open, inside was a letter.

"Its' time to meet: 315pm at 1415 Warehouse Rd. You want the answers, you want the truth. Come by yourself, this is as difficult for you as it is me. This can be as hard as you want to make it. If I wanted you dead you would already be dead. The dreams and the nightmares will soon come to and end. Your mind and my mind are the same, we have the same nightmares, and we have the same dreams. I need this to end. For that to happen we have to meet. You'll be relieved to finally know the truth.".

Guess Who?"

Amanda read the letter, it didn't seem as bad as she expected. It sounded like he was much the same as Cal and wanted this all to end.

"It sounds like he wants to confess," she said reading the note.

"You can't meet him, only me," Cal told her.

"You can't meet him Cal" her eyes wide with fear.

"I have to end this thing Amanda" he paused "It has to end now before it's too late".

"If I don't I'm going to go crazy" he added simply.

They argued that for a while longer. Amanda thought he should get the police involved. Cal finally convinced Amanda that he had to find the answers alone. She wanted to go with him, but he refused to let her. They finished breakfast and went back to the room. They concentrated on finding out where Warehouse Road was. That was the easy part finding a map of Miami. They finally found the street map and the street he had to go too. It was down in the harbor, dockyards. Cal had to do this alone and had to find out the answers he had been searching for so long. He knew he should have taken a weapon with him, but refused, if this killer would have wanted him dead Cal would have been dead along time ago. Cal knew the only solution was to do this alone.

He wondered about Mundale and if he had any luck at the Hammond Penitentiary. It was already getting close for Cal to go to the warehouse. Amanda did not want to see him leave and thought that he should wait or get the police involved. Cal said he would know and then he wouldn't show up. He had to do this alone and he had to do it now.

Detective Mundale sat in his room, he hoped the judge would call again soon with some good news. He knew that Tom Keene, the old man was almost 83 now. His health was failing and he feared for his life. The phone rang at the same instant starting Mundale.

"Mundale here" he answered, waiting for some good news.

"Jim, Judge Munro here" the judge paused "Got some bad news for you" he hesitated. "Tom Keene is dead"

"Tom Keene is dead" Mundale said his voice suddenly quiet.

"How?" Mundale said his voice shaking, knowing somehow that Warden Sims was involved.

"Warden Sims called this morning, apparently Keene died in last night, in his sleep," the judge told him.

"That's horse shit Pete!" Mundale said using the judge's first name "He's covering up for the old man's death".

"Don't know apparently they found him this morning dead in his cell" Judge Munro explained.

"I smell something rotten" Mundale said point blank.

The judge agreed telling Mundale not to worry there would be a proper investigation. He went on to tell Mundale that one of the guards found Tom Keene after he didn't come out of his cell. The Warden claimed there was no one else around at the time. They said they would do an autopsy on Tom Keene. State law requires an investigation and autopsy into the death of any person dying from an unexplained death.

However, they will probably claim that he died from old age and that none is required.

Mundale hung up the phone flabbergasted by the death of Tom Keene. He knew now that he was definitely onto something. Someone wanted to cover up the Devil's Brotherhood and keep Tom Keene silent. Mundale now wanted an investigation into Hammond penitentiary. Especially, Warden Sims. He knew that Hammond was a maximum-security prison; it would be difficult for him to get access to the files of such a facility. He had to find out what his next move would be. Mundale knew this whole ordeal of unsolved murders; the Devil's Brotherhood and Tom Keene's death were connected. But, how they were connected he didn't know.

Detective Jim Mundale knew that he didn't have much information, what he did have wasn't enough to warrant a full investigation. He had to work fast and find more information on the death of Tom Keene. Maybe, the autopsy, if one were even done, would warrant further investigation. If and when the day came he also knew the FBI or penal systems would be involved. He was concerned that the death of Tom Keene was connected to the Warden, and if that were the case then the he would have a difficult time proving it.

He picked up the phone dialing. "Room 1616" he asked.

It rang a few times before Amanda Riley answered. He was surprised to hear her voice and not Cal's. He was worried that they may do something foolish and be in danger.

"Miss Riley, is Cal there?" he asked, "Its Detective Mundale calling".

She explained to the detective about the note and that Cal had went to meet with someone on Warehouse Road. He could tell by the sound of her voice that she was worried and distraught.

"Why the hell would he do that!"? Mundale went nuts "How and the Hell could he be so stupid".

"I tried to stop him, or at least call the police," she told him. "But, he wouldn't, he said he had to do this alone" she went on "He said if the police or anyone else got involved it could jeopardize everything".

"How long ago did he leave?" Mundale asked, wondering if he should get a hold of the Miami PD.

"A little over an hour ago" She said her voice had a worried tone in it.

Mundale knew it was too late to do anything now. But, he had to try; he hung up the phone and called the Miami police department. He briefed a detective on the situation and gave him the address.

Cal Rushton had little trouble finding the address he was told to meet at. The taxicab pulled up in front of an abandoned building. It was a four-story old brick structure. It appeared to have been long vacated. Windows were boarded up; it's dark and empty shell looking ominous. He stared at the building wondering what was in store for him. He had second thoughts but immediately dismissed them.

"Give me one hour, if you don't hear from me by then call the police" Cal told the cab driver throwing a one hundred dollar bill to him.

"Sure thing buddy" the cabby said as Rushton walked towards the building.

Cal went through the front door of the building. His heart pounded in his chest, he realized this man could kill him. This man was a killer and for some reason wanted Cal alive. He entered a small room, which at some point in time was used as an office.

Broken glass crunched under Cal's heel, as he looked at the graffiti sprayed walls. Broken glass was everywhere, light streamed into this room through an open window. The room was entirely empty except for an old wooden chair. He looked at another doorway going out into the empty warehouse. He went through the opening cautiously looking around the huge room. There wasn't anyone in sight. This room was covered with broken glass and bottles. Cal stepped into the center of the room. He could feel he was being watched but for some strange reason didn't feel threatened.

"Hello" he said loudly, the voice echoing in the empty space.

No reply, he repeated "Hello" his voice echoing through the empty building.

This time a voice came from the dark shadows of the room.

"You're alone?" the voice of the man called back, the voice didn't sound threatening in any manor.

A match lit, the man lighting a cigar from the blackness of the room. The man's face vaguely seen. He was wearing a black over coat, and a black brimmed hat. His stature told of a big man with broad shoulders.

"Yes" Cal responded watching the shadow step into the light of the dimly lit room.

"First of all, I'm not here to kill you" the voice showed no fear as the man stepped closer.

Cal strained his eyes trying to get a better look. He couldn't make out the face of the man in the shadows.

"Who are you?" Cal asked as the man stopped 30 feet from him.

"It's not important who I am," the man told him tugging his hat down, puffing on his cigar.

"Don't jump to conclusions, you may be surprised with the truth" the man replied, his voice seemed confident.

Cal stepped forward, suddenly he wasn't afraid of the man. It must have been the tone in his voice, but he didn't fear any danger. He wanted more than anything to find out who he was.

"You want the truth," the man said taking off his black brimmed hat.

Cal stood listening as the man explained who he was and the story behind their meeting. He stepped closer to Cal they were now only a couple feet from each other.

"You are what I've been waiting for. You see what I see and what I feel. My real name is John Natas," the man said rolling up his sleeve and revealing a tattoo on his arm.

The man looked to be in his fifties, the tattoo on his arm was The Devil's Brotherhood. The number 799 was engraved in the center. Cal listened as the man explained and went over the story.

"It all began for me in the summer of 1974. I was 21 at the time; it was a hot hazy summer day. That was the year I became reckless and did the things that still haunt me today. I belonged to a Detroit street gang. To make it short we had a feud with a rival gang. In those days gangs were just a phase. We got into a gun battle with the rival gang. A rival gang member killed my best friend at the time in the battle. I totally lost control and hunted the rival gang members down. In the end I killed a rival gang member, beating him to death in his own apartment.

I was convicted and sentenced to 20 years. It was a stupid thing to do at that age, but I was young and didn't know any better. As well I got mixed up in something that was way above my head.

I was sent to Hammond Maximum Security Prison. That's the year I met Hank Crossling. We were sent to Hammond the same year. We became friends and were virtually inseparable. In the prison was much like life on the streets. Gangs formed and fought for power over the rest of the prison population. We formed our own gang along with a couple of other prisoners we looked after each other. A member of one of the other gangs approached us.

That gang called themselves the Devils' Brotherhood. At that time there were very few that knew of the brotherhood. It wasn't until we were tattooed for the gang that we got the real meaning. I was initiated first my number 799 was followed by Hank's number 802. The next thing I knew one of the other new members Tom Keene got the number I was curious as to why the numbers skipped. It was told to me then why the numbers and their significance. It was the number of deaths credited to the Devil's Brotherhood. So the reason it skipped a numbers between Hank and me was that he had been convicted of 3 murders. We thought it was funny at the time. But the years went by and new members were brought into the fold.

In the 80's Hank and myself were now the gang leaders. The numbers rose slowly and at my time of parole in 1989 the number was approaching 2000.

A man known as Solomon started the Brotherhood back in 1964. He apparently, had killed six people in a rampage. He blamed it on racial discrimination, he being black. The first four or five years only black convicted killers were invited into the Devil's Brotherhood. But in 1970 the first white man joined the brotherhood. The man battled

Solomon and gained the respect of Solomon. The racial tensions died in the prison system until the death of Solomon in 1974. The same year I came to Hammond.

The man, Lucas Smith that had battled Solomon for his respect took over control of the Devils Brotherhood. As Smith got older his life became threatened and he passed the reins to Hank Crossling in 1980. Hank ran the brotherhood when I was released in 1989. I'm not sure if he was still in charge at the time of his death or not. All I know is that in 1996 shortly after his death, I was hunted by the brotherhood.

On the outside world life was good for me. Hank Crossling let me run his business ventures. At the time of his death, the businesses were handed down to me. He left me millions of dollars, to be exact 15 million dollars. In 1996 one of the brotherhood members contacted me. He told me Hank was dying in prison and that I should see him. Hank Crosslings death was the death of John Natas. That is my real name, he confessed. The man wanted to meet with me and make arrangements to see Hank Crossling, who was on his deathbed.

I met the man in an abandoned warehouse, much like this one. I thought it was suspicious but I met him. The man was hidden in the shadows; he jumped out behind me burying his knife in the small of my back. I turned to face my assailant. He loped off my right ear with the blade of his knife. He laughed and left me for dead on the floor. I thought I would die, but somehow I managed to crawl out of there. Somehow, I crawled to my car and called my business partner at that time. An ambulance arrived; the last thing I remembered was the feeling of falling. I woke up in a hospital bed three day's later.

The assassin didn't finish the job he was sent to do. I nearly bled to death and the near death started haunting me. It haunts me like it haunts you. I managed to change my name and cash in my holdings, handing them over to my partner. I picked up the pieces and had the good fortune of having an honest business partner. But in 1999 that changed when he was murdered.

He was murdered much in the same way that I was attacked. The killer took his right ear and stabbed him to death. The police came after me for the murder of my partner. I once again was forced to pick up and change my name. I had visions that were shared with Colin Ray Barker. I assume the reason I had those visions were because of his involvement with the Devils Brotherhood. The visions were of murder, nightmares of the worst kind. I tried to entice Barker the same as I did you. I had to play it safe, I wasn't sure if Barker had the intelligence to help me put the puzzle together.

Barker wasn't bright enough to carry forward what I was trying to do and that was draw the Devils Brotherhood out and expose the killer amongst them.

"Barker died in prison," Cal told him, unsure if he knew.

"He didn't die the way you think he did, he was murdered," he told Cal.

"I have some questions I need answered?" Cal asked Natas, wanting to know the rest of the story.

"I'm sure you do" John Natas replied.

"The ear of Eva Tucker, did you send that to me?" he asked him waiting for his reply.

"The ear of the victims is a calling card for these lunatics" he paused "You see this is a conspiracy, a conspiracy to get the wealth left behind by Hank Crossling" he stopped.

"I was close to the killer of Eva Tucker, I almost had enough visions to stop what was going to happen" he told Cal "But he figured it out or should I say they did and I was too late. "I followed the man I suspected to Miss Tucker's home. I tried to stop him, but it was already too late. Your visions were not as clear as mine were. I see what you see, and that's why I had to meet you.

These killers know you don't forget it. But, what these men are really after is me. They want to protect the brotherhood and as well get the wealth left behind by Crossling. You're probably wondering why I didn't go to the police. The truth is tried, but I don't know whom to trust. The brotherhood is bigger than you think. They reach into the outside world and corrupt people that we think are honest. The killer draws me out through you. There is someone that sees the same as we do, when we find him, we stop our nightmares. Until then our nightmare continues.

The Devils Brotherhood, which was at one time a small prison organization, has hit the main stream of society. Once an unwritten secret prison society, now it's just a killer's trademark, a society that involves politicians, lawyers and law enforcement. It's a corrupt society that has many illegal activities. The one that leads and now controls has to be stopped.

"Who is the leader?" Cal asked stunned by the story he was hearing, and unclear as to what his own envolement would be.

"Its someone that has great influence" he paused "Someone with enough power that he would almost be impossible to stop" Natas finished. "The same man that is responsible for the deaths in the outside world. This man that controls his band of killers takes the right ear of their victims as proof. It started with me," the man said removing his hat for the first times showing the missing ear.

"But what about the ear of Eva Tucker" Cal asked him.

"That was my doing, I arrived at Eva Tuckers almost in time to stop the killer from killing her. That is why she survived, her ear was already cut off, and the damage already had been done. I managed to struggle with the killer and scare him off.

I sent the ear to you along with the strange notes to see if you could put the puzzle together, and to see if you could be trusted.

"I know that sounds bizarre and strange, but where Barker failed you have come this far" The Brotherhood still knows I'm alive. The main reason for all this is to get what they believe belongs to them, That Is Hank Crosslings Empire. If they succeed in that, there will be no stopping them. Hank Crossling's wealth has grown.

Today the estimated wealth of the Crossling Empire is estimated at forty million. The man that owns that empire is me. I inherited that money, built the businesses and invested the money. With Hank Crosslings brilliant mind from behind prison walls the empire grew stronger. My identity has been changed and hidden very well. I have a few good people working for me that I can trust. He told Cal.

"I still don't understand what does the killer and Crosslings Empire have to do with each other". Cal asked still confused by what he was hearing.

"The boss of the Brotherhood is trying to draw me out to claim Crosslings Empire. These individuals have to either kill me or have me sign the empire over to him.

The last couple of years in prison, Crossling was tortured, beaten, and threatened Hank Crossling signed a waiver that in the event of his death his holdings would be turned over to someone. The problem is I'm still not sure who that is. Having learned from an inside sources my partner and I had another document drawn up. This legal document entitled me to Hank Crosslings Empire. But, the legal glitch was the document, null and void in the event of my death. No one knows the identity of the new boss of the Brotherhood. I have a hunch who it might be, but I still need further proof". Natas told him.

"What do I have to do with all this?" Cal said accepting Natas story but still confused.

"First you have to protect yourself, by letting the killer know your working with me. In order to do that you have accepted the gifts I've given you. Spend the money on things that you want. Remember they are always watching you. He knows that I'm beside you and wants to draw me out. Someone has the same visions as us; the only difference is they are using theirs to get to me. When he thinks you have led him to me, he will kill you and Amanda". He paused, turning and walking away into the shadows of the big room.

"Be careful and beware," he warned.

"Wait, how do I contact you" Cal replied just as the man disappeared.

"There will be a package at the front desk of the hotel" he said shadows of the room.

Cal Rushton stood, shaking his head at the bizarre story. He turned walking out of the building to the waiting taxi.

"Just about to call the cops" the cabby said as Cal got into the back seat of the car.

Cal didn't respond to the driver. He looked over his shoulder at the run down building looking for some sign of the strange man and the strange encounter. The man called Natas didn't want him dead after all, he wanted Cal's help to draw out the Devils Brotherhood and the killer.

Detective Mundale wanted an investigation into the death of Tom Keene. He wanted it now, and he wanted something done. He wouldn't stop until he was satisfied with the answers. He was sure there was something about Keene's death that warranted a full investigation.

Judge Munro's home was an old Victorian home on the outskirts of Fox Creek. He drove there now having come back from Hammond empty handed. Mundale was mad as he drove into the yard of the huge Victorian home. Judge Munro was expecting him as he rang the doorbell. Alice Munro, Judge Munro's wife answered the door. Judge Munro agreed with Mundale that he smelled something fishy about the whole Tom Keene thing. He also told Mundale it would be hard to implicate Warden Sims, but that an investigation was in order.

"Mr. Mundale, I assume" she smiled sticking out her hand.

"Yes" Mundale said excepting her handshake.

"Peter's expecting you in the sitting room" she said escorting him down the hallway full of gorgeous art exhibits.

The home was a huge old estate inherited by Peter Munro. He had let his wife furnish the home to suit her tastes. Mundale complimented her on the beautiful home and her decorating skills. They entered the well-lit library that also was Judge Munro's office.

"Jim, how you doing?" Munro said getting up from his wing-backed chair.

"Anything to drink?" Munro asked him, knowing that he would probably need one after all the events of the past day.

"Scotch on the rocks" Mundale said as Alice Munro left the room.

Munro preceded pouring himself and Mundale a drink.

"Do you have anything?" Mundale said referring to the Hammond prison.

"Yes, but its not much" Munro said sitting down and handing a drink to Mundale.

Munro had managed to get access on all the prison records. Every inmate since the institution was established in 1963. They were particularly interested in Tom Keene's file.

"Tom Keane was put into Hammond in 1968. He began reading the notes he had "He was quiet when he first came, there were no incidents on his report. But then in the summer of 1970 he spent some time in solitary confinement. That same year the kingpin of Hammond Penitentiary, Solomon Burke spent time in and out of solitary as well. Apparently, Tom turned out to be tough nut. It doesn't mention much after that. Relatives and his wife only visited Keene a few times. The last visitor Keene had was in 1986. He seemed to be a loner and kept to himself, especially near the end.

"Anything about the Devil's Brotherhood" Mundale asked.

"Not a thing, it's as if they didn't exist" the judge told him passing Keene's file to Mundale.

Mundale opened the file briefly searching Keene's file.

"Your good friend Warden Sims came to Hammond in 1994. He came from another institution in Michigan". The judge told him.

"Redwood Maximum Security Prison" Mundale read out loud.

"Maybe, we should investigate Sims" Mundale said not liking the man one bit.

"On what grounds Jim?" Munro warned.

"I don't know, just got a hunch about him" Mundale retorted.

They sat discussing the details on guards, prisoners, etc. They came up with nothing on illegal activity. They could find nothing on the Devils Brotherhood. Detective Mundale had in the back of his mind Cal Rushton and what he was up too. He wondered if Cal had found anything or if he was even still alive. Mundale was ready to strike out at Warden Sims; he knew that the death of Tom Keene was Sims doing. He stared at the glass of scotch taking the last drink. Munro was busy looking for a way to have a full investigation into the death of Tom Keene and especially Hammond Penitentiary. Detective Mundale looked at his watch realizing he should try and contact Cal again.

Cal Rushton arrived back at the motel, exhausted and confused. He was yet to find anything that had a tale like the one he had just heard. The whole thing seemed impossible to imagine. So this stranger wasn't the killer, then who was? How could he flush this man out? John Natas had told Cal to draw him out by spending money and that would convince the killer that he knew John Natas. Maybe, if he had time to do some research he could figure out more about John Natas.

It then dawned on him that Mundale was waiting for him to call. Maybe, Mundale had some information by now that would help. After all he knew the date of release of John Natas. He knew the man was in his fifties.

Cal went to the front desk and asked the desk clerk if there was anything for him. John Natas had told him to go to the front desk; there would be something there for him. The clerk came back carrying a brief case. The tag hanging off it had Cal's name on it. He thanked the clerk and made his way onto the elevator. A man got on the elevator with him. He was wearing a short-sleeved shirt. The man said nothing, but instantly alarms sounded in Cal's head. The man looked suspicious and waited for him to get into the elevator before the doors closed. Maybe, his mind was running overtime because of the whole thing, but still this man seemed mysteriously suspicious to him.

"How are you today?" Cal asked the man, checking his arm out for a tattoo.

"Well" the man responded, in an off mannerism.

Cal decided he was just being paranoid as the man got off on the sixth floor. The man brushed Cal on the way off the elevator. The door slammed shut as Cal suddenly had a vision. Cal saw the man's face in his vision, he heard the scream of a victim. Then it was gone as quickly as it had come. Cal thought about Amanda waiting for him. If anything were to happen to her he would rip that mans heart out. He ran off the elevator and panicked running down the hall. He turned the key in the lock and the door opened.

Was the man already in Cal's hotel room while he was out? Amanda sat on the sofa looking at him, when he entered. Tears were in her eyes, she had been crying. He thought maybe she was concerned that something had happened to him.

"What's wrong Darling?" He said running over to her side.

"It's nothing," she said trying to hold back the tears.

"Oh, its something, what is it?" Cal asked again.

"It's my business, the bank is going to foreclose on it," she said looking out the window.

"That's it!" Cal said relieved that was all.

"It might mean nothing to you, but to me it's all I have" she said offended by his remark.

"Sweetheart, it will be okay" he smiled

"I don't have that kind of money to pay them off before they foreclose. "How can you say that?" she asked starting to sob again.

Cal got up from the sofa and went into the bedroom carrying the suitcase with him. He opened it, in shock at the money inside. He was amazed that this man John Natas had this kind of money to throw around, and why would he on Cal.

"How much do you need?" Cal said showing her the briefcase.

"That's not your money," she told him

"It's my money to do what I want to with" Cal stopped and explained briefly about the money that John Natas had given him.

Cal forgot about the man in the elevator and his concerns over the killer. He was elated that he could help Amanda with her problems.

"I still owe the bank sixty thousand dollars," she told him.

"Call them now" he told her "Get on the phone and call them".

She gulped tears drying up. She hugged him and kissed him. She was overwhelmed that he would bail her out of trouble.

"Anything for the woman I love" Cal said realizing that he was professing his love for her.

"I love you too," she said smiling, realizing what she was saying it before it even left her lips.

"I have been since the first night we stayed together," she confessed.

Cal told her to call the bank and they would wire the money to the bank. She picked up the phone as Cal reached for the briefcase. Cal opened it his jaw dropping open. Inside was more money than he had ever seen. A gun was also in the briefcase and a letter.

He showed Amanda just as the phone began to ring.

"Oh my God" Amanda said hanging up the phone.

"How much do you think is here" Cal wondered.

Cal knew he had made a promise to John Natas. One he had to keep, unless he wanted to be haunted the rest of his life. He opened the envelope reading the letter inside.

Cal:

If you're reading this letter you have decided to meet with me. The fact is I have had a man watching you leave and another one watching the warehouse. The choice you made to meet me shows me you're a man of courage. It tells me that you have what it takes to carry forward to the next step. The world you're stepping into is dangerous and deceptive. No one can be trusted. I need you to do one thing for me. In this suitcase is five hundred thousand dollars.

I want you Amanda to go to the Casino Royale on the North side of town tonight. You will have the reason when you get there. I have my sources telling me there is a former inmate of the Brotherhood running the place. His name is Roland Sutherby he will recognize you. I want you to take one hundred thousand dollars and throw it around. Before you get there I need you to make a stop or two. There you will buy a new tuxedo for yourself and a new gown and jewelry for Amanda.

Look the part of a millionaire. I want you to buy her anything she wants and for yourself as well. This money is a token of my appreciation to help me get over these visions and nightmares.

Money is no object for me. The gun is registered in your name. I want you to take protection in case we lose you. I will have a half dozen men and one woman waiting. The woman will approach you at the craps table. She will ask you to rub the dice for good luck. You can't miss her she's my wife. Don't worry your in capable hands. This has to end before any more lives are lost to the Brotherhood. If we take down the leader once and for all, it will die with him.

Thanks

John Natas

Detective Mundale sat in his office waiting for a phone call from Cal Rushton. He was worried so he picked up the phone dialing the number. Cal picked up the ringing phone. Cal was thinking about all the money and all the wealth he had now. He could take off right now with the money and never have to worry again. But, it was as John Natas said if he did the nightmares and dreams would only continue and escalate.

"There's a call for you Mr. Rushton, do you wish to take it" the clerk asked.

"Put it through" Cal said hoping it was Mundale.

"Cal is everything okay?" Mundale inquired, worried about the last conversation he had with Amanda.

It's okay, but very hard to explain on the phone" Cal said worried about the phones.

"It exists Cal, I know it does" Mundale told him.

"Yeah well buy me one in yellow," Cal said trying to get the detective to understand.

"Yellow?" Mundale responded not clueing in to Cal's response.

Cal was trying to throw the conversation off so no one understood what was going on. He didn't want Mundale to jeopardize his life as well as Amanda's.

"I'm willing to pay one hundred and fifty thousand dollars, if you meet me at the Armada Hilton tomorrow morning at 11am. Cal said trying to get the detective to Miami.

"Okay tomorrow morning 11am at the Armada hotel, got it" Mundale said understanding the there must be a reason for Cal to talk like that.

Amanda waited for Cal to get off the phone before asking him any questions. She sat looking at the money in the briefcase reading the note.

"Cal, I'm not so sure about this" she said still nervous.

"We'll be safe, I promise" Cal said assuring her safety.

"Did you call the bank yet?" Cal said closing the suitcase.

"No" she said tears welling up in her eyes.

"Amanda, call the bank, it's okay darling I love you," he said putting his hand on her face.

"But I don't want you to end up like Colin Ray Barker" she replied, referring to what Pearl Barker had said.

Cal reassured her that wouldn't happen. He told her that her shop means a lot to her and she meant a lot to him. Finally, she called the bank telling them she would have the money in full, by the end of the business day. She hung up the phone happy with the outcome.

Cal was certain that everything would be okay and that the visions and nightmares would end with the end of the Devils Brotherhood. The fact still remained that he was in danger as was Amanda. He thought about his brother Bobby. Bobby was not in very good shape financially; maybe he should send him some money. If something were to happen to him at least Bobby and his family would benefit from it.

They prepared for their night out at the Casino. Cal and Amanda had to look their best to convince Roland Sutherby that they indeed had access to a lot of money. Cal was still curious as to why John Natas had reached out for him. With his wealth there was probably another way to approach these men of the Devils Brotherhood. He would have to figure out why later, right now it was time to prepare for the Casino.

Cal and Amanda arrived at the casino in style. Amanda was dressed in a stunning red sequenced gown; complete with a fur coat and of course jewelry hanging off her. Cal looked at her in the back of the limousine, leaning over and giving her a kiss. This was like a dream to have this much wealth and have a beautiful woman beside him as well.

"A man could get really used to this," he said smiling at her.

"Your not so bad yourself" she smirked.

"Don't worry honey, everything will be fine" Cal said with a note of confidence.

The doorman opened the door of the limousine. Cal got out extending his hand to the beautiful Amanda. Other people stopped on the street to watch the couple. They were a handsome couple people were looking in awe. They must be dignitaries or movie stars. The couple walked into the casino arm in arm. Casino personnel acknowledged the couple opening doors and greeting them.

They walked in the casino and down the elegant steps into the lobby of the Casino Royale. Cal slid the briefcase onto the counter wicket. An older man greeted him.

"Good evening sir" the man said watching Cal open the briefcase.

The man's eyes widened as Cal opened the briefcase and asked for one hundred thousand dollars in chips.

The man hesitated picking up the phone.

"Sir could you give me a couple minutes?" the man asked, checking with his boss as he was told to with any big spenders coming into the Casino.

A couple minutes later a big well-dressed man appeared behind the counter.

"How may I help you sir?" the big man asked.

"I would like one hundred thousand dollars in chips" Cal said opening the briefcase again.

"I'm the manager of the Royale, my name is Roland, sir," he said sticking his hand through the wicket.

Cal reached through to accept the big man's hand. He realized it was an instant mistake. A vision of this big man assaulting a young woman came into his head. Sutherby suspected something being wrong when the blood drained from Cal's face.

"Everything all right sir" Sutherby asked, realizing that Cal was suspecting something.

"It will be" Cal responded gritting his teeth at the feeling he just had.

Roland Sutherby's attendant was busy getting a tray of chips ready for Cal.

"Any preferred denomination?" Sutherby asked.

Cal rhymed off the denominations he wanted and bid Roland Sutherby a good night, proceeding to the gaming tables. Roland Sutherby watched Cal cross the room to one of the gaming tables. The evil in the man's eyes was quite evident. He was part of this whole thing and a member of the Devils Brotherhood. Hopefully, Natas people would be here watching closely at what was going on and get them out of trouble before it started.

"Amanda, I want you to stay close to me, but I want you to play" he told her.

"Pick a game," he suggested. Looking around the huge gaming room.

"Craps" she said without hesitation.

They saw the craps table and proceeded to make their way to the table. Cal looked around the table, noticing a very beautiful woman. Perhaps in her early forties he guessed. Maybe that was John Wells's wife. He acknowledged her on the instinct she was John's wife.

"All bets down" the attendant said handing the dice to an elderly man.

The man rolled seven red, Cal won. He left the chips on the table to the pile. Cal moved his chips on a hunch, and won again. The attendant added more chips to Cal's pile. Cal lost a couple times in the first half-hour. The chips in front of him now were roughly twenty thousand dollars.

Cal watched the gaming attendant carefully wondering if he was another member of the Devils Brotherhood.

"Would you like to roll" the Attendant asked Cal.

Cal took the dice, noticing the woman come closer. He placed his wager again. Now he had doubled the money in front of him. He placed his bet again as the woman made her way beside him.

"Kiss for good luck" she said in a sweet southern accent.

Cal held out his hand as she kissed the dice. He rolled

winning again. Now there was a huge pile of chips in front of him.

John Natas wife stood closely by as if waiting for something to happen. Amanda stood by patiently, as Cal decided to ride the entire pile one more time. Crowds of on lookers now gathered watching the chips pile up. He took half the pile again moving it to another spot. This time he lost, but at least it looked as though he had won fifty thousand dollars or so. He decided to try his luck elsewhere looking carefully around the room.

"Not bad" Cal said picking up the chips, handing the beautiful one a five hundred-dollar chip.

"That's for good luck, would you care to join us?" Cal asked, smiling at her.

"It would be my pleasure," the charming woman said.

"I'm Doris," she said introducing herself to Cal and Amanda.

"I'm Amanda," she said smiling and instantly feeling at ease with beautiful Doris.

Doris was gorgeous and stood out amongst most women.

She was very classy, her beautiful blue eyes, soft warm complexion and blonde hair made her a very attractive woman. The three of them made their way to the Black Jack table. Amanda excused herself to go to the washroom. Doris joined her as they made their way to the washrooms. Amanda was comforted by Doris and felt at ease and safe with her.

Cal hung around the Black Jack table waiting for a free spot to open. He looked around the room noticing Roland Sutherby standing talking with a big black man. The man worked at the casino, it was apparent by his dress. The black man had massive arms and hands, which he had folded in front of him. Cal felt the cold stares of the two men. They were watching his every move. Cal took an empty seat at the Black Jack table suddenly feeling very comfortable.

Amanda went into the empty stall while Doris checked her makeup. Doris waited until the bathroom was empty before speaking. She was still nervous by the situation and wanted to know what would happen next. Cal seemed to fit right in to the part he was playing and had the confidence to do so.

For Amanda it came much harder to pretend she was something she wasn't.

"Are you having a good time?" she asked Amanda, waiting for a response.

"I'm nervous, but I feel much better now that you're here" she told her.

"Tell Cal only be here a couple hours then go back to the motel" Doris told Amanda.

"Will they follow us?" She asked referring to Sutherby and the brotherhood.

"Were hoping to force them to play their hand," she said putting fresh lipstick on.

"I'm sacred, but not for me, for Cal. He's been through a lot with all this," she said flushing the toilet.

"You're a very beautiful young woman, I can tell you care a lot about him" Doris said trying to ease her anxiety.

The two finished in the washroom and made their way back to Cal. Doris made sure that she made Amanda feel more at ease and not to worry they had men at every corner watching out for them. Cal sat playing Black Jack his luck had turned bad. He was losing quite a lot of the money he had won. Although, he was still up, he asked Amanda to take a turn while he got a drink. She was reluctant but with a nod from Doris she decided to give it a try.

Detective Mundale sat in his office, he was tired and dreaded to turn in for the night when the phone rang. He answered the phone stunned by the voice on the other end.

"Detective Jim Mundale" the man replied.

"Yes" Mundale said.

"There's been a murder, I think you had better come to the Munro house as soon as possible" the voice said again.

"Who is this?" Mundale asked as the phone clicked, whoever it was didn't identify themselves.

Detective Mundale was stunned by the news. But, he was even more confused by the voice on the phone. This was another warning to back off. Maybe, he should just do that and get back to his home. Then he thought of Cal Rushton, maybe Cal had better news than what he had found. The Devil's Brotherhood covered their tracks well. However, the Devil's Brotherhood never really made their impact on the outside world until lately.

Mundale slipped his shoes on locking his hotel door. He left heading back north towards Judge Munro's home. He wondered if this had just been a ploy to get him out of the hotel room. He had no sooner got the thought out of his head than he saw bright lights of a vehicle baring down on him. The vehicle was now on his tail, he could tell by the size of the vehicle that it wasn't a car. The vehicle flashed its bright lights in Mundales mirror. Suddenly it rammed into the back of his car. Mundale swerved almost losing control of his car. He reached for his gun as the vehicle was hit again. The gun slid off his lap onto the floor by his feet. The jolt crumpled the trunk of his small car. The car hit the shoulder of the road, Mundale fought for control.

Mundale got the car back under his control as the four-wheel drive truck pulled up beside him. Mundale hit the brakes the truck swerving to hit him. He had little time the truck speeding up behind him again. He fumbled around on the floor looking for his 38 special. The truck was now in front of him. The truck jammed on its brakes, Mundale smashing into the rear of the truck. Mundale hit his head on the steering wheel. He saw the flash at the same instant the shotgun blast blew out the windshield of his car. He felt the sting of glass, and the sting of the pellets hit his face. He raised the 38 special just as the second blast took him in the right shoulder. His car went off the road rolling over in the ditch.

Mundale lie unconscious as the truck backed up. The truck stopped for a few seconds, a passenger started to get out when a set of headlights came down the highway. The truck sped off leaving Mundale to die in the wreckage of his car. Mundale watched the headlights disappear and the new headlights of another vehicle approaching. His only hope now was that whoever was coming down the road would stop and get him out of the wreckage. He felt the blood on his shoulder and touched it gingerly. Then the detective passed out.

Cal Rushton managed to lose nearly twenty thousand dollars as he cashed in his remaining chips. Roland Sutherby came over watching him and Amanda closely. He picked up the phone talking in a rushed voice. Cal was at the wicket watching Sutherby closely talking to someone in a hushed voice.

Cal and Amanda got into the limousine. He looked around the parking lot looking at all the cars and guessed that in one of those cars was a couple of men belonging to John Natas. Cal still knew that Sutherby was watching closely and this was far from over. The plan according to Natas was to draw the men out in the open and get to the bottom of everything.

"Where to sir" the limousine driver asked turning over his shoulder.

"The Hilton" Cal said referring to the hotel.

The limousine sped off down the main streets of Miami. Cal had an uneasy feeling watching the flicker of the city lights in the distance. Amanda sat silent, she was more nervous now than she had been at the Casino. For some reason the both of them felt something was going to happen.

Chapter VIII
The Truth Revealed

The driver of the limousine took a strange route the cars behind flashing lights. Cal looked back out at the flashing vehicles. He knew something was up and waited for the driver to make a decision.

"Hey driver where are you taking us?" Cal said tapping on the window. The driver of the car said nothing pulling the car off onto another side street. It abruptly came to a stop at a row of large empty buildings. Stepping out of the shadows were six men. Amanda sat terrified as the driver of the limousine got out of the car. The cars came to a stop behind the limousine.

Cal opened the door of the limousine. This was it the standoff they were waiting for, but where was John Natas and his men. Was this all just a setup by Natas to get what he wanted, to have them off his back and blame Cal.

"Stay here" he said to Amanda, taking the gun out of his waistband.

The men from the shadows lined the sidewalk, waiting and watching. Cal got out of the car, four men came up from behind Cal showing up from the shadows. Doris followed the men; she made her way beside Cal. Relief flooded Cal's mind when Doris arrived.

"Amanda come with me" she said opening the car door.

John Natas appeared standing beside Cal. John Natas didn't look intimidated and held a gun in his hand ready for whatever was to happen next.

"This is where we find out what they want," he said looking at Cal.

It was a standoff, with no one saying anything. A big man appeared out of the shadows.

The man appeared to be the one they were waiting for to show up. It had come down to the standoff without much fanfare. But, the electricity was evident in the air and something was going to happen within the few next minutes.

"Alright, Natas, this is the way it is" the big man told him. "We want twenty five million and the whole thing stops here," he demanded.

"I wish it was as easy as that, but your gang of killers won't stop it will just get stronger" Natas said not backing down from the big man.

"We've finally found out where you are, it's only a matter of time before we find out how to find where you live" the big man warned.

They started forming a circle around Cal and Natas. Amanda got into the car with Doris watching the standoff. This was going to be a fight and there was no doubt about it. The men of the brotherhood began to spread out and surround John Natas.

John Natas didn't flinch he held his ground.

"I've got something you want" Natas said indicating twenty million dollars. "As long as I breath, the Devil's Brotherhood is why I still get up in the morning. I'll stop you killers if I die trying" Natas barked.

Suddenly, without warning the gang charged in. Natas men weren't caught flat footed. John Natas fell back when the brawl started. He tugged Cal on the sleeve pulling him back from the melee. His men were out numbered, more men from the brotherhood appeared. It was evident this was where the trap was to be sprung. The only thing about it they were out numbered by a lot of men. Natas and Cal made a run for it, getting into the car with Doris and Amanda.

"Damn it" Natas said watching his men get beat up.

"Go Go" John said telling Doris to drive.

The brotherhood was making their way towards the car. Doris smashed into one of them sending him flying. John Natas reached inside his overcoat pocket taking out a gun. Doris floored the car speeding down a one-way street. Other cars were now in pursuit. Buildings went by in a blur the car speeding above the speed limit. Suddenly, they hit an intersection; they were no sooner through the intersection than two cars blocked the road they just came through. The drivers bailed out of the cars just as the lead car smashed into the roadblock. A huge explosion followed flames lighting up the sky.

Cal turned in his seat watching in horror the explosion, ripping the cars apart. It was John's men blocking the way and risking their lives to save John Natas. Cal suddenly felt the excitement rising in him to an all time high. He had only seen stuff like this in movies.

"Holy shit" Cal exclaimed.

"So it begins" Natas sat with an expressionless face.

The silver Cadillac being driven by Doris disappeared onto the ramp of the busy interstate. The car slowed down to the speed limit. Doris seemed cool, calm and under control. She reached over with her free hand taking Amanda's hand. She could tell that Amanda was about to lose control with her emotions.

"It'll be all right sweetie," she told her.

Detective Jim Mundale was at death's door in the emergency room. He had taken a shotgun blast to the right shoulder. Some of the fragments were embedded in his face and arms as well. Luckily for him the full blast didn't hit him. He had taken quite a few of the pellets in the upper part of his body. His face was bandaged, and his shoulder was bandaged as well. Mundale was just now waking from a three-hour surgery. He was groggy but remarkably still alive.

Detective Jim Mundale vaguely remembered the voices of the people who found his wrecked car with him inside.

"Where am I?" he said looking at the nurse hovering above him.

"You're in recovery sir" the nurse responded taking his blood pressure.

A plain clothed police officer entered the room.

"Detective Mundale can I ask you some questions" the clean-shaven tall officer asked.

"Yeah" Mundale said feeling woozy.

"Do you remember what happened?" the officer asked him.

"Vaguely" Mundale said trying to fight the wave of pain.

"Where were you going?" the officer asked.

"Judge Munro's" Mundale said his head starting to fill with darkness.

"Judge Munro and his wife were murdered last night," the officer told him.

"What?" Mundale said in disbelieve

"Let him rest now" the nurse said seeing his blood pressure go up.

"Devils Brotherhood" Mundale whispered as he fell into unconsciousness.

The young officer heard the words his eyes getting big with the mention. Officer Cody Lane had heard the name of the Devils Brotherhood mentioned before. He had thought the whole thing as a myth or a tale. That was until his own experience as a rookie with a member of the Brotherhood changed that. He was working a case with a senior officer on an unsolved murder case. The senior member of the force mentioned he thought the Devils Brotherhood were responsible for the killing. He remembered the young girls, raped tortured remains. The girl had disappeared from her parent's home a week before. The father of the young girl a well to do politician offered a reward. The officer in charge of the investigation had come up with a lead. But, the night they were supposed to meet and discuss the suspect the senior officer was killed in a bizarre accident. Lane thought about that case from time to time. The case went unsolved and this was five years later. Maybe, there was something to this Devil's Brotherhood after all.

Lane left the hospital telling the nurse that when Detective Mundale was awake and alert he would like to be notified. Lane headed back to the office to go over the five-year-old murder case, and to see what Mundale was working on at the time of the shooting. Lane was young and green but he still was highly intelligent and remembered what happened to his partner three years previous after mentioning the Devils Brotherhood. It was much the same as Mundale the only difference was his car was driven off a bridge with him in it. They claimed suicide at first, but after some persuading by Lane they reduced it to an accident. All along Lane suspected something more but was never able to put his finger on exactly what his suspicions were.

Cal and Amanda were driven north of Miami for a half-hour, outside the city limits. The car pulled into a rich looking neighborhood. It stopped outside a huge gate, in the background a mansion sitting on a hill. The house looked under heavy security. The security guard at the gate let the car in.

They pulled to a stop on the cobblestone drive. They entered the huge mansion into the foyer of the mansion. The home was well decorated and well lit. A butler came and took their coats. John Natas led them into a huge sitting room. The room was full of 1800's furniture. Hung above the fireplace a picture of John and Doris. John looked tired and worn his only concern now was for this all to end. What they had started this time he was bound and determined to end.

"Now that the war has begun," Natas said sitting in the huge wing backed chair. "The Devil's Brotherhood will be out for more blood, than they ever have. The only way of stopping them is to find out whose behind the organization. I'm afraid that we will see some very powerful and influential people in charge of the brotherhood". He said clipping the end off a cigar.

This was the first time Cal had seen Natas in the light. The handsome man sat in the chair thinking. His beautiful wife

Doris sat on the side of his chair rubbing his hair. They were a very handsome couple. She was trying to comfort him through all the things that had happened. It had almost come between them on a couple of occasions, with Doris threatening to leave unless things changed. However, she knew she never could leave him. Doris loved John and it was evident by the pampering she was now attending to him.

"What do we do next?" Cal asked.

The place was a well decorated home with a lot of antiques and valuable things.

"Now that we know Roland Sutherby's apart of this thing, we get to him" Natas said without hesitation.

Two men appeared in the doorway. The two were from the brawl. One man held an ice pack on his head; the other had one eye nearly closed shut. The man with the nearly closed eye spoke. They were beaten badly, but then again they were also out numbered badly.

"Sir we got away, glad your safe" He said concerned for the well being of his boss.

"What about the other men?" Natas said getting up as Doris went for the first aid kit.

"All accounted for, but a bit worse for wear," he confessed as Doris came back in leading two more men to the sofa. "One of the men might not make it, but other than that we were lucky to get out alive" he confessed.

Another woman came in dressed in a maid's uniform. She brought towels a tub of hot water and face cloths.

"Where are the others" Doris asked concerned about the other men.

"In the hospital, they weren't as lucky" He told them; "a lot of broken bones and fractures".

"Cal this is Jake, he's our chief security man around here," Natas said looking at his bruised man.

Amanda and Doris went out of the room. Doris took Amanda upstairs in the home. John Natas, Cal, Jake and the other men sat in the room deciding what to do next. John Natas knew that the next move was in the Brotherhood's court. He knew that it was only a matter of time before they found him. The brotherhood was waiting for their break to find the infamous John Natas. Now they knew he was alive, and the chances were in Miami somewhere?

The next step was to confront Roland Sutherby and get the information they needed from him. It wouldn't be an easy task. Especially, with Sutherby's gang of thugs watching over him. Natas men were to watch the Casino Royale. The men left leaving Natas and Cal alone.

"Do you trust your men" Cal asked point blank.

"Yes with my life, I have treated them and their families very well, they would die for me" Natas stated.

John Natas decided he had better tell Cal the rest of the story. He proceeded to explain to Cal about his visions and nightmares. He explained that Cal that he had his own visions and nightmares since his own near death episode. Natas own nightmares and visions got stronger when Colin Ray Barker started having them. Barker's face was in his mind and consumed what he was seeing. Finally, he found Colin Ray Barker who was working for his brother in law.

Natas tried to figure out why he was sharing his visions with Colin Ray. There had to be some kind of connection between the two of them, but what? He hired men to investigate Colin Ray. He thought Barker was the murderer at first, then after Colin Ray's arrest for murder an investigator came to him. He told him some strange information. Colin Ray's father now deceased had been convicted of murder. His father was sent to Hammond in 1968. His stay was brief, Vince Barker, Colin Ray's father died in Hammond in 1970. The death of Vince Barker was a mystery. It was rumored that he was murdered, but again no proof was found. Vince Barker was rumored to have threatened to kill Solomon at the time. He was singled out and killed for not wanting to participate in the Brotherhood.

"But I don't have any connection with the brotherhood" Cal said questioning the reasoning.

John Natas paused not sure if he should go on or not. Cal sensed his nervousness. He could tell that John Natas wanted to tell him the rest but was unsure if he could handle the rest of the truth.

"What is it? Cal asked the hair on the back of his neck standing up.

"Your Hank Crossling's son" He told him point blank, heir to all that you see.

Cal sat shocked by the news not knowing what to do. He thought his father had died along time ago, but didn't know he was in prison.

Detective Mundale woke up in the hospital bed. His groggy head, couldn't distinguish what had happened. The heavily sedated detective tried to think of what happened. A nurse came into the room noticing him alert and awake. Mundale's chest hurt, his head was throbbing but he was mad, upset someone had tried to kill him and also upset that probably the same ones had managed to kill the Munro's.

"Oh, your awake" she said taking his blood pressure.

Mundale said nothing he stared off into space trying to piece together all the strange events. He wondered if his wife and children had found out about the accident. Then it suddenly dawned on him that an officer had been in talking to him.

Mundale vaguely remembered the young man but remembered Cody Lane being there.

"Was there a detective in here?" he asked the nurse.

"Yes, Mr. Mundale, he left you his card" the nurse said picking up the card on the nightstand.

"Could I please have a phone?" he requested.

Cody Lane, Mundale said it out loud sounded like a Hardy Boys character.

"Are you sure your strong enough" the nurse asked.

"There's something that could mean life or death, if I don't talk with him" Mundale told the nurse.

The nurse left the room arriving several minutes later with a phone. Mundale went over in his mind what he had said to Lane. Did he hear it right that Judge Munro and his wife were murdered? He dialed the number.

"Detective Lane" the officer replied.

"This Is Lieutenant Mundale calling" Mundale said.

Cody Lane asked Mundale if he felt well enough to talk about what happened.

Mundale told him that he had to tell him about the case he was working on. He told him simply he wanted him to take over for him. Mundale told him to get his files on the case and his contact list.

It was a matter of fifteen minutes when the young detective Cody Lane arrived to see Mundale. Mundale went on to tell him the bizarre tale of the Devil's Brotherhood. Lane sat in silence listening to the older officer tell his story. "The Devils Brotherhood is real!" Cody Lane said after Mundale was done. He always suspected that there was more truth than speculation regarding the Devils Brotherhood. Now at long last the truth was coming out.

"Yes, I'm afraid that Cal Rushton and Miss Riley will be next. That's unless you can get to Miami". Mundale told him the story giving him complete access to all the files for the case.

"Your wife knows you've been hurt," Lane told him "She's coming in to see you at three" he finished.

Detective Mundale was exhausted by the explanation of the bizarre tale. He felt his eyes getting heavy. Mundale gave Cody Lane the phone list that he carried with him. Lane would fly to Miami to try and find Rushton. He left the hospital as Mundale drifted back to sleep.

Cal Rushton sat stunned by the news, unsure what to say to John Natas. This was the connection, as bizarre a connection as it was. Was his own father communicating to him? He still had wondered why it was all happening to him, but now he had some kind of explanation as to why John Natas would want him as an ally.

"How could that be?" he finally said.

"Your mother was embarrassed by the murder conviction that your father got," he told him "She went into the adoption program and gave you up for adoption. You were very young at that time and would have no recollection of your real father. That is why you have this curse of the Brotherhood that it why you have these visions and nightmares.

Your journey to here has been hard Cal; I know you didn't feel like you fit in anywhere. Now you know why you felt that way. It had nothing to do with the rest of the family, they were all told never to tell you that you were adopted. It was for your own safety. Your brothers and sisters don't know the truth about you, for that matter your mother didn't know either. Your stepfather, the man you thought was your father started to find out where you came from. But, when he got close someone had to shut him up. I still don't know who had him silenced but I suspect it was someone that wanted to keep your identity safe.

He told Cal the story. Your mother was not Crossling's wife, in fact they were going through a divorce so he could re-marry his real love, your mother. But, when he got blamed for their deaths, she decided to give you up. She feared for your life as well. Cal had a look of disbelieve as Amanda and Doris came back into the room. She noticed the shocked look on his face and wondered what had happened.

"What's wrong Cal?" Amanda asked him, noticing the distant look in his eyes.

"I'll be okay," he told her not to worry her.

A loud commotion was heard in the hall. John Natas jumped to his feet to see what the commotion was about. Some of his men came into the room with Roland Sutherby. His hands were tied behind his back and he was furious. His face was beet red, he was cursing and going on like a wild man. They had managed to capture him and bring him to Natas. They laid in wait for Sutherby to make a wrong move and he did just that.

"Well Well" Mr. Sutherby, to what do we owe the pleasure?" Natas said

"You sons of bitches better let me loose now, if you know what's good for you" he threatened, his temper evident.

"Now, Now Mr. Sutherby, I think we control the situation

here don't you" Natas said his tone suddenly harsh and mean.

"Tell you what Sutherby, you tell us what we want to know and we can let you go" Natas told him.

"You won't get shit from me" Sutherby said his eyes bulging with anger. Sutherby was a big brute of a man had his alliance to the Brotherhood he would never jeopardize that.

"We will see about that," Natas said pulling a gun out of his drawer of his desk.

"John!" Doris exclaimed a look in her eyes that told them she had never seen this side of him.

"Doris, take Amanda and get out of here," he told her his voice a rough raw tone in it.

Doris and Amanda left the room, Doris shaking her head over his tone.

"Now I know you won't shoot me" Sutherby snickered, looking down at the barrel of John Natas gun pointed squarely at his chest.

John Natas walked up to Sutherby holding the gun low. He pulled the trigger, Roland Sutherby's leg caved. The neat hole in his kneecap blew away by the bullet from John Natas' gun. The gunshot echoed throughout the home. John Natas had no pity for Sutherby and his actions with the Devils Brotherhood. He would just soon kill him as anything. The men held him up as Sutherby screamed in pain. Cal had never seen anything like it; he was shocked by John Natas. Sutherby started whimpering, when John Natas cocked the trigger aiming at the second knee.

"You going to talk or do I have to waste all these bullets" Natas said a pure look of rage in his face. "Or you can be a cripple the rest of your life as far as I'm concerned".

Even the men in the room were shocked at the violence that John Natas was showing.

"Fuck, I'll tell you what you want to know" Sutherby said, knowing that Natas would kill him just as soon as blink an eye.

"Who is your boss?" Natas asked, pulling the hammer back on the weapon.

"I don't know his name, he just calls me when he needs me" Sutherby said.

"Bullshit" Natas said taking aim at Sutherby's head.

"I'm telling you the truth," he sputtered.

"Give me a name Goddamn it" Natas glared.

"Senator Logan" the man said.

"Logan" Cal said, "how could that be his daughter was killed by you people?" he said.

"Yes, because she was a disgrace to him and his political campaign. Sutherby told them.

"Another name, then we can see what we can do about that leg," Natas told him.

"Warden Sims" Sutherby said, implicating Hammond Penitentiary.

"You mean the Warden of Hammond penitentiary?" Natas asked.

"Yes damn it now fix my leg," the man moaned.

John Natas waved his gun for the men to take him away. He simply strolled back over to the sofa and sat down. He sat back thinking about Logan and his influence. He would be a hard cookie to crack, but somehow he would. Natas never would give up until those guilty were brought forward and punished for their crimes.

"Okay so we got a Senator and a Warden, I wonder how many more there are to this" Natas said.

"Jesus John, you mean Logan had his own daughter killed?" Cal was shocked at the caliber man that Senator Logan was.

"It takes all kinds of greedy people, who would stop at nothing to get what they want Cal". The sooner you learn that the better off you will be. Greed comes in all shapes and all disguises. Greed is heartless, ruthless and has no feelings towards other living souls," John Natas said.

"So what do we do now?" Cal asked.

"We go after Warden Sims, hit him where it hurts" Natas told him.

"And where would that be" Cal asked.

"That would be in his own prison, all it takes is a phone call," Natas told Cal who sat in awe at the man's cool approach.

John Natas picked up the phone dialing a number. His voice was hushed but Cal could hear what he was saying.

"Phil, its Natas here" he said to the other man on the phone. "Warden Sims, make him talk, make him squeal, I don't give a shit what you do, I want two names" he said hanging up the phone.

"What about Logan?" Cal asked.

"We do nothing about him, we drag him in for the killing of his daughter, we get a confession from the man who did the deed". Natas told him. "We drag him into the prison system and let him pay his dues" Natas said.

Cal Rushton sat listening to the plan. It seemed to be a good plan if it worked. But, the thing was who could be trusted and who couldn't?

Warden Sims sat in his office feeling smug that he had taken care of Detective Mundale. Unsuspecting the plans that were for him. In Hammond Natas had allies and many of them. He thought how the man had tried to interfere with prison business.

The killing of Tom Keene had been swift. One of his henchmen carried the dead out while the old man was asleep. He died without so much as a whimper. He had covered the tracks of the Devil's Brotherhood once and for all. Now he could see no outside interference.

He sat talking on the phone to one of his contacts explaining that the job had been taken care of. Suddenly a knock came on his door. Warden Sims had given strict orders not to be disturbed.

"Hang on a second, someone's at the door" he grumbled.

"Who the hell is it?" he said raising his voice.

"It's a detective Lane to see you sir," the guard said.

"Got to go, someone's doing some snooping here" Sims said hanging up the phone.

Lane came into his office carrying a file folder full of information.

Lane was confident that he could get to the bottom of the Devil's Brotherhood. He didn't know the capabilities of Warden Sims. Sims was ruthless and would stop at nothing to protect the brotherhood. He had quite a nest egg from the Brotherhood's dirty deeds and was going to let no one come in the way of that.

"How can I help you?" Warden Sims said looking at the young officer with contempt.

"I want an explanation as to why there wasn't an autopsy done on Tom Keene, and why he died? Lane said in a cocky tone.

"I owe you know explanation" Sims said sarcastically standing up from his chair.

"I think you do sir" Lane said throwing the file on his desk.

"What the hell is this?" Sims said raising his voice.

"Its evidence that you murdered Tom Keene" Lane lied knowing he didn't have enough evidence.

"That's bullshit boy, now get the fuck out of my office and out of my prison" the irate Sims stammered.

"Not until you explain to me, what did Tom Keene die from and why wasn't an autopsy done" Lane said not backing down.

"I owe you no explanation and unless you have a court order I wont talk to you anymore" Sims said picking up the phone to call security.

"I'll be back with a court order," Lane told him, thinking of Mundale and what had happened when he tried to interfere.

"I also think you had something to do with Judge Munro's death" Lane stated.

A security guard showed up at the door. The guard looked at Warden Sims then at Lane.

"Show this asshole out of my office and out of my fucking prison" Sims said really getting irate.

The guard escorted Lane out of the prison. Cody Lane wasn't about to give in to Warden Sims. He would just keep digging until he was satisfied. He was like a pit bull with a grudge. After all Mundale was critically injured in a shooting, Tom Keene was dead, and Mr. and Mrs. Munro had died. He felt the urge to walk back into his office and demand answers. But, declined thinking better of it until he got a court order. He wanted to get Sims but he had to do it right.

Sims sat in his office, he was furious. How dare that young pup come in here and try to tell me how to run my prison. How dare he come in here making accusations about murder? He thought he had all the bases covered until Lane walked into the office. Another knock at the door.

"Now what?" Sims was still upset, there was no calming him down.

"Got some problems in cell block D" the guard told him.

"What kind of trouble?" Sims barked.

"Some of the Men are rumbling about the Devils Brotherhood, while others are standing up to them. A brawl sir, they attacked the guards and have taken over the cafeteria"

"They say they want to see you about conditions in the prison" the guard told him.

"Oh for fuck sakes, do I have to do everything by myself" Sims said following the guard out of his office.

The guard escorted Warden Sims down to the D block. He stopped as they turned the last corner, looking at Sims.

"Why are you stopping you dumb fuck?" Sims said looking at the guard.

The guard turned around as two inmates showed up from around the corner. What was happening here, Warden Sims felt in control up to this point.

"What the hell is this?" He barked his authoritative voice.

"Its payback time Warden" One of the inmates said grabbing him by the collar.

"Get your hands off me, I'll have you in solitary for a month" Sims threatened.

"Not this time Warden" the other man said, a smile cursing his lips.

A third man came around the corner, the two others holding his arms. Warden Sims dirtied his pants when he realized they meant business and it was payback for all the lousy treatment they had received in the past.

"Let me go" he squirmed; fear now replacing the usually calm demeanor.

The third man hit him in the stomach, the force expelling the air out of his lungs.

"We need some information Warden," the man told him, enjoying finally being able to get to the Warden on his own terms.

"What do you mean?" Sims said fear in his eyes.

"We need to know who you take your orders from?" the man said kicking Sims in the kneecap.

"From the Government" Sims said trying to cover up.

"No from the Devils Brotherhood" the man snapped hitting him again this time square in the jaw, breaking two of the Wardens teeth. He began to bleed profusely.

"Please, I don't know what you're talking about" Sims told him.

"Hold him down," the man said, pulling out an iron bar tucked in the back of his prison uniform.

The two other inmates held him down forward his face facing the floor. The other inmate came up with his knee breaking Sims nose, blood squirting onto the floor.

They waited a couple minutes for him to come back around.

"Talk you bastard," the man said his voice in a rage.

"Alright I'll tell you what ever you want to hear" Sims finally gave in.

Sims told the men what they wanted to hear. He gave them two names; one was a bigwig judge, the other city mayor. The Warden crumpled in a heap the three inmates putting the boots to him. Warden Sims wasn't a very well liked warden. His time had come in the prison system. These men would make sure that he would never be the same again.

Cody Lane managed to get a flight to Miami. He checked into the Hilton hotel waiting to hear word back from Cal Rushton. The clean-cut officer was a very clever man.

He had been working on a lot of cases involving homicide in the past couple years. Now he had to find Rushton and solve the mystery behind the Devil's Brotherhood. He thought about Mundale and his near death episode. Was it just a bunch of false leads? Was the Devil's Brotherhood really responsible for the deaths of Judge Munro and Tom Keene? He searched for details about the crime scene. It was clean; both the Munros had been shot once in the head. Both had their right ear cut off.

The phone rang in his room, it was Cal Rushton.

"Detective Cody Lane here" Lane answered the phone.

"This is Cal Rushton" Cal spoke clearly; he knew it had to be some news about Mundale.

"What's going on?" Cal asked finding out about Detective Mundale.

"Mundale was attacked, shot and driven off the road," Lane told him.

"Is he okay?" Cal asked worried about Mundale one of the few men he honestly respected.

"He's serious, but he will make it" the detective reassured him.

"Any leads?" Cal asked.

"He said the Devil's Brotherhood, but that is just a myth" Lane told him.

"It's not a myth," Cal said, waiting to tell Lane the whole truth.

"I have no proof that it exists, do you?" Lane said, questioning Cal.

"Yes I do" Cal said, getting a bit irritated with Lane.

"Could you meet me at my hotel room?" Lane asked him.

"Yes, when would you like to meet" Cal asked him.

"Your choice, but could you bring along your proof?" He asked Cal.

Cal told him okay hanging up the phone a bit confused by the young officer's line of questioning. He told John about the officer and about Mundale who had been injured. He went on to tell him that Mundale was honest and helping him to figure things out. John Natas became suspicious of Lane, by the line of questioning aimed at Cal. He didn't trust anyone after all there were Judges, Senators, and Wardens involved.

"I'll go with you" Natas said. "What time?" Natas asked.

"I told him within the next hour" Cal responded

They managed to get something to eat. Doris and Amanda were getting along nicely. Cal still couldn't believe that he was Hank Crosslings' son. It was a lot of things that he had learned the past couple days that had him totally dumb founded. The Devil's Brotherhood, Jim Mundale, His finding out about Hank Crossling, all was very confusing to him.

Cal and John Natas left for the Hilton hotel. The ladies stayed behind, happy to be away from the confusion of the past few days. They arrived at the motel, Cal felt nervous for some reason about meeting

Cody Lane. John Natas was as cool as always, nothing seemed to shake the man. They went to Cody Lanes room, knocking on the door.

"Cal" Lane said waving them in at the doorway. "Detective Cody Lane" the brash young officer said.

"I brought along a friend that can help me clarify my story" Cal told him as they entered the room.

"Hello sir, now if you two would like to grab a seat let's get down to this" Lane said getting right to the point.

"I have Detective Mundale's file here," he said pointing to it on top of the dresser.

"Did you see anything strange in it?" Cal asked. "It was a bit confusing to me, it didn't seem to make any sense" Lane said getting up heading towards the dresser.

Suddenly, John Natas had a look in his eyes of worry. He sensed something was wrong. His fears were answered when the bathroom door swung open to a man holding a gun.

"You see Mr. Rushton, we do know the answers already" Lane said a smirk on his face as he turned from the dresser a gun in his hand.

Cal was speechless, he had fallen for Lane's story and come here hoping that he was as honest as detective Mundale. He had figured that Lane was honest knowing Mundale's authority and trust.

"Why?" Cal responded.

"You see Mr. Rushton you almost had it figured out, the only thing missing was the killer of those poor defenseless girls" Lane smiled, implicating himself.

"You son of a bitch" Cal said knowing that Lane was confessing to the murders.

Lane nodded his head for the other man to come into the room.

"Why thank you Mr. Rushton, or should I call you Crossling" Lane said his tone changing to one of contempt.

"I've been working for the Brotherhood for three years, trying to track down the mysterious John Natas. "Now I not only have him I have the son of Hank Crossling. Its such a bonus to have both the men that could benefit our brotherhood so much" Lane said referring to the enormous wealth that Hank Crossling was connected too. "Do you realize the important people that are waiting for me to finish the job here?" Lane said tooting his own horn.

"I can only imagine" Natas replied, trying to reach his gun stashed in his coat.

"Let's just say that I have become a very valuable member as well as very rich from this." Lane said, he would not only become wealthy but would be free to kill again.

The other man didn't move he stood there holding the gun on Natas. Without warning Natas moved lightning fast. He waited for the other man to take his eyes off him for one second. When he did he reached for the gun inside his coat and grabbed it. Lane fired the bullet digging into Natas' side. Natas got his shot off and on the mark taking the other man dead in the center of the chest. The man toppled forwards falling onto the floor. Cal moved quickly during the commotion just as Lane fired his second shot. This shot went into Cal's left arm. Cal was in mid air when the bullet struck home. He felt the burn, but still managed to hit Lane with the full force of his body, knocking the gun out of Lane's hand. John Natas stood up holding the gun in his hand over Lane now lying on the floor.

Lane looked up at them "Now what are you going to do" he still seemed to have his cocky attitude towards the whole ordeal.

"Turn you over to the proper authorities, or maybe I should just shoot you" Natas said harshly waving the gun in a threatening manner.

"And say what, you don't have any evidence" Lane said knowing fool well he had an alibi. I have a clean record, I'm the law here, its my word against yours" Lane said confidently.

"Like I always say trust no one" Natas said pulling out a tape recorder from his inside pocket of the coat.

Lane's jaw dropped open he didn't respond he laid there in quiet anticipation of the next 50 years in prison or the death penalty. Lane had confessed to the murders and to being apart of the Devils Brotherhood.

The ordeal came to a close; the nightmares had finally stopped for Cal and for John Natas. The days that followed brought forth many high-ranking businessmen, attorney's, judges, and politicians. John Natas had suffered a shot to the lower left abdomen and would be okay in the days that followed. He and Doris turned the money over to Cal who after all was the descendant of Hank Crossling. Cal didn't want all the money instead he left all his business with John and Doris and only took a portion of the money.

Cal and Amanda got married a year after the ordeal and moved to southern California.

Tom Keene's body was cremated before officials could respond. There was no charge in his death, only the speculation that rose from it.

Warden Sims seemed to have disappeared; no one knew where to find him. There was a rumbling within the new brotherhood that Sims body is buried in the confines of the Hammond Prison. They said he was beaten to death by inmates and buried by guards at the institution. No investigation followed it was all a matter of here say.

Jim Mundale retired with his family and moved back to Rhode Island to be closer to his wifes family. He eventually got well enough to start his own business venture, backed by John Natas and Cal Rushton.

Politician Logan was subsequently found guilty of conspiracy to commit murders and sentenced to a 35-year term.

Cody Lane waits on death row for an execution time to be set. His involvement and taking the lives of four victims was finally solved. Those were the four that he confessed to, it was also rumored that Lane was responsible for considerably more deaths. He stated in his statement the only reason he killed those girls was to cover up the Brotherhoods involvement in the outside world and to have a cover for The death of Kathleen Logan, ordered by her own father.

The murders of Judge Munro and his wife have yet to be solved. But, there is speculation that the brotherhood has come forward with leads for the investigation. They were laid to rest with Mundale and Rushton at the funerals.

The Devil's Brotherhood still functions today, although it has cleaned up its act considerably. The brotherhood now reaches out to those less fortune. The Hammond prison inmates are directly involved with fund raising and charitable donations. That's what they say, but who knows what other dealings the Brotherhood has.

Printed in the United States
111598LV00002B/127-135/P